BARB WIRE

BARB WIRE

MARIE FORD

The EC Publishing LLC books may be ordered
through booksellers or by contacting:

EC Publishing LLC
116 South Magnolia Ave.
Suite 3, Unit F
Ocala, FL 34471, USA
Direct Line: +1 (352) 644-6538
Fax: +1 (800) 483-1813
http://www.ecpublishingllc.com/

Ordering Information:
Quantity sales. Special discounts are available on quan-
tity purchases by corporations, associations, and others.
For details, contact the publisher at the address above.

Printed in the United States of America

I would like the public to understand that the same individuals that commit crimes whether it is robbery, assault, child molesters, kidnapping or murder, once they are arrested, they may sit in the county jails for month to a year. They are eventually brought to a prison facility for safekeeping, while awaiting court. We as Dept of Public Safety / Corrections staff must deal with these individuals daily. You as the public feel safe because, these people have been removed out of society and place in lock up, but we as trained professional will have to deal with these individuals, not knowing a lot of times what could happen. There are inmates that deny the crimes they are accused of to come to prison. These inmates have already been in front of a Judge and Jury in a court of law. Once they arrive at the Facility, we are responsible for the Safety and security of that inmate as well as protecting ourselves and the public. We are not there to Judge Inmates. There is a lot of staff that want to know what this one and that one done. I did not want to know. I did at one time start keeping Scrap books newspaper clippings of individuals that committed crimes or you would see it on the news. When I saw their faces, I would be familiar with them. There are some inmates that would come to you and talk about their crime(s). I would sit and listen with no feedback. You watch Television you see where people have been released from prison, because it was found that they were innocent. This is after they have spent most of their life in prison.

We as Dept of Public Safety encounter individuals that come from all walks of life; there are times that we come in contact with individuals that will cause harm to us and themselves. We have to do what is necessary and appropriate to protect all involved. We as people observe or hear things and make the wrong interpretation. When this happens, we all are made out to be the bad guys. Most of us want to do our jobs and be good at what we do. I am sure there are several books out here that talk about prison and what happens on the inside, but everyone has a different outlook and different experiences. There are some that have had bad experiences and are very negative. It doesn't matter what job you work on; you have always got to weed out the bad or rotten apples, unfortunately there are many. Though out this book you will be able to understand when I say **all walks of life**. The individuals that myself and co-workers had to encounter on a day to day basis. You will see inserts of crimes committed as I went **Though the Rank.** There was also a documentary done by **MSNBC LOCK-UP.** You will also see throughout the book, there were books, movies and other documentaries about the female population.

2005

They seemed to be the perfect couple, two college students smart, driven and in love. They moved to North Carolina in 1993 to attend graduate school and after graduating, he became a pediatric AIDS researcher and she was a chemist. Their relationship became strained and they fought over money. Then an affair came about with a coworker. November 2000 a plot came about to poison the husband with arsenic from the lab she worked. The husband beer was dosed with arsenic during a bowling outing and became sick. He was hospitalized several times before dying. The wife continued the dosing until he died. The wife was sentenced 25-31 years in prison. This case had been the subject of a book "Deadly Dose."

2000

Defendant was charged with first-degree murder of her fiancé. The State's evidence tended to show that on the evening of 28 March 2000, The Police Department responded to a call about a shooting at a house. The defendant's thirteen-year-old daughter let the officers into the house when they arrived. In the bedroom at the end of the hall, the Officer observed the victim lying on the floor on his back, face up, and defendant lying face down, across the top of the victim. The defendant was wearing a white wedding gown. She was moaning and moving her hands and arms across the victim's face. When defendant rolled over, police discovered a revolver next to the victim's face. The victim, who had blood coming out of a hole in his shirt, had no vital signs. The front of defendant's wedding dress had a black powder burn and blood on it. The defendant appeared to be bleeding from a gunshot wound to her lower left breast area and was transported to the hospital. Police did not find signs of forced entry into the residence. At the scene, police observed a gunshot hole through the headboard of the bed, a gunshot hole in the closet, and a spent projectile laying flush against the headboard and baseboard of the floor. Police collected a

2

brown wig, a wedding veil, beads, a revolver, four spent shell casings, and two live rounds from the bedroom.

State Bureau of Investigation testified that the bullet retrieved from the victim's abdomen during the autopsy, the bullet found at the scene, and the four shell casings retrieved from the scene all came from the revolver found at the scene of the shooting. The State Bureau of Investigation, testified that the findings of the gunshot residue analysis on the victim's hands were "not consistent with the firing of a weapon." Police determined that defendant was a specialist in the Army Reserve and a security guard.

The Chief Medical Examiner for the State of North Carolina testified that the victim died as the result of a gunshot wound that struck the aorta. He further testified that the lack of gunshot residue around the victim's gunshot wound indicated that he was shot from several feet away.

On top of the bedroom dresser, a note read: "His soul was tired, so I gave him a rest and I loved him so much I went with him. Love, me." In a dresser drawer, police found an unsigned marriage certificate dated. The detective found a calendar with the following entries: "My wedding day, "My babe's, husband's 60th birthday." The victim's daughter testified that her father was engaged to defendant. The defendant and the victim had been living together in the victim's home along with defendant's children for about a year and a half. The defendant and the victim had set wedding dates in the past and the next tentative date. The defendant was in the process of buying the wedding dress.

The defendant did not present any evidence. A jury found defendant guilty as charged. The trial court sentenced defendant to life imprisonment.

November 2008 the victim's body was discovered at the home of the defendant. Family members had become concerned that they had not seen this child since the holiday. They had asked the defendant about the child and the response was she had been keeping him away from certain people. CPS was contacted by family in which the defendant refused to talk to CPS. The family went to the residence and discovered the child's body in a closet. The victim was in a plastic bag containing sheets, which had been soak in bleach to mask the smell of the body. The police were notified. The defendant told police that the child was jumping on the couch and fell. The def did not report the incident due to being afraid of the father. An autopsy was performed that showed ongoing abuse. There were broken ribs found in various stages of healing. She made a statement about beating and kicking the victim. It was determined the victim had been deceased about 6 weeks. Due to the decomposed condition, the cause of death could not be pinpointed. The defendant was convicted by a jury of 1st degree murder and failing to report the death of the 19-month-old victim.

There was a time when we cared about what we say, do and how we look, now it has been put on a shelf and stored away somewhere along the way collecting dust. There was a time when you go to an interview on a job, you go looking sharp, like you wanted the job. When you see people come in now, they are dressed any kind of way. I've seen them come in with shorts and tennis shoes WHAT!!! First impressions go a long way, just because a person has degrees does not mean that job is for them. Common sense will be the best sense you will ever have in life, being honest and having integrity will be the 2nd best thing. No one wants to deal with a dishonest individual, it will not get you far, you will be hiding and skating under the radar all the time trying not to be found out, who wants to live like that. Hey, some people get a thrill or a rush out of it, unfortunately. Most of us live by examples that have been set for us whether they are good or bad. You always make the best of what you have at the time and something better will come along, it may be sooner or later depending what situation, you are in at the time, sometimes you can do better with **less** than, you can with **more**. Always CYA (COVER YOUR ASS) and never ever **ASSUME.**

There are a lot of staff that do not respect the uniform. I've seen the entire uniform on sale on the internet. You have your uniforms on, going into the shopping malls, grocery stores. Unless you are going in and coming right out, don't go to these places with the uniform on. You have to be mindful of what's going on around you at all times. Inmates get out and they are living life like we are. They may notice you without the uniform and they may come up, speak and let you see they are free. Then there may be one that don't like the uniform, not you but the uniform for whatever reason. There was a time that some staff were killed, when they stop to get gas or stop at this store. They were killed by some ex inmates, because of their uniform, it was the understanding they didn't know this staff. Speculation was that the individuals were not treated fairly, while incarcerated. They targeted the uniform not the staff wearing it. Always remember none of us are perfect, by no means and the inmate you mistreat could be you or your family member, always treat people the way you would expect to be treated.

In this business you have to love what you do and do what you love. You just can't be in it for the paycheck. You can, but you will be miserable and unhappy negative towards the job. This was not good because you would make the staff around you miserable and unhappy as well. This job may be good for some but not good for others. One thing for sure two things for certain, you have to have the mind set to work in the Department of correction. This job was not made for everyone! The old saying was its not the inmate that will cause the problems, it will be the staff. That has held true down through the years. You have your good staff that are pretty much worked to death. Then you have you're not so good staff, that complains and whine about everything, just causing problems. (earth disturbers) Then the good staff have to make up for what the problem staff don't do. Therefore, causing problems in the workplace. You have staff that abuses the system using different types of issues to sue or get workers compensation. These same people are working other jobs or out of work going their merry way and still getting paid. Then there are staff that have been truly injured on the job like me and put through the 3rd degree about their injuries and given a hard time about workman comp. The turnover rate is so high. It was hard to keep individuals on board. Some came only to receive a paycheck, at the end of the month. I say again you got do what you love, and love what you do. Some were in school majoring in criminal justice and need the credits or hands on experience and they did not stay either. The new hire's that came in, some looked as if they would be good candidates for this type of work. We would give the basics. You can lead a horse to water, but you can't make him drink it. You can give a person all the tools to use to do their job, but you can't teach them common sense. You could have all the book sense, college education you want, but when it came to dealing with offenders and your peers, people you supervise, your common sense has to show up. I remember the year the work first crowd was being hired, this was the worst thing for state corrections, because most of the individuals didn't want to work. They mostly did it to show they had tried to work, so they would not lose food stamps and assistant from the Social Services. This one person that was hire had been given access to a vehicle to go to Basic Training. Later it was found they were using the vehicle for their own personal use and had been seen at the laundry mat SMH.

1997

The defendant did feloniously commit the offenses of murder second degree and assault with deadly weapon w/ intent to kill inflicting serious injury. According to the detective of the police department, there was an altercation two week before the crimes occurred. A group of girls came to the defendant's residence. The victims involved were not present at this altercation, but it was about one of the victims. The defendant was dating one of the victim's friends. A group of friends came to the defendant's apartment to talk to the defendant about some rumors had been spreading. The group had a long talk and supposedly things were straightened out. One morning some friends were washing clothes at a laundromat, when they saw a vehicle come by that the defendant was riding in. The defendant was staring at them as they rode by and had apparently left. The defendant and her friends came back and followed the car as they were leaving. The defendant's car cut through a parking lot to make a left turn. The vehicle cut the defendant's car off and almost ran them into a telephone pole. When the cars stopped everyone got out, but they did not fight because there were more people in the defendant's car. At that point everyone decided to leave. Later that day, two were on their way to the apartments to

pick up some friends to go to the mall. As they got out of
the vehicle, they saw the defendant standing at her door and
began arguing with her. One of the defendant's friends, was
there and got into a fight. The defendant stated, "let me get my
shoes," and stepped away from the door. A few minutes later
they came out the door at of the apartments holding a silver
revolver and began shooting. As the victim was running,
she was shot in the back. One of the shots from the handgun
also struck a victim in the arm. The victim died soon after
the shooting. Another victim was hospitalized, received an
operation, and a pin was placed in her arm. Detective had no
findings of drugs or alcohol in the case.

on august 15, 1997, The defendant was convicted of murder
in the second degree and was sentenced to a minimum term
of 189 and a maximum term of 236 months department of
correction. The defendant was also convicted of assault with
deadly weapon with intent to kill inflicting serious injury.
The defendant will serve a term of 100-129 months at the
expiration of the first case.

2002

On the morning of February 15, 2002, a 23-year-old young lady and two of her girlfriends had been drinking wine on Valentine's night and decided to play a prank on the ex-boyfriend by pouring some clam juice into the car's fresh air intake so that a foul odor would result when the heater was operated. The young man's car was not in the parking lot so it was decided that she would set a fire to a box of party decorations and an old futon as a prank outside her former boyfriend's college walk apartment in North Carolina, It was a windy night, the fire quickly got out of control on the wooden breezeway of the wooden apartment building, and it set the apartment building itself on fire, resulting in the horrible deaths of 4 innocent people. The two other girls with her the night of February 15 were not charged. They hired lawyers who went to authorities with their version of what happened in prepared statements. This young lady nor either of her two friends called 911, banged on doors to awaken sleeping apartment residents, or did anything that might have saved lives or prevented injury. They panicked, as anyone may in a situation gone far beyond control. This doesn't excuse their actions, but it perhaps makes their behavior somewhat easier to comprehend, she was facing prosecution under a little-known law called the felony murder rule, which states that if a person commits or attempts to commit certain felonies, in this case arson, any deaths which may result from the felony are charged as first-degree murder. Intent to commit murder does not have to be proved, and there are only two possible penalties after being found guilty under the felony murder rule: death, or life in prison without possibility of parole. The law also holds that any persons with the perpetrator of the felony must also be held accountable in the same manner as if they, themselves, were perpetrators of the felony and prosecuted accordingly. She was threatened with the death penalty if she did not plead guilty.

Barely more than a college girl has been convicted under North Carolina's version of the felony murder rule, the most powerful criminal law on our books, which is normally reserved for hardened sociopaths, repeat offenders, and other offenders who show no comprehension or conscience. Unless something extraordinary happens, she will die in prison.

2004

In the incident victim was visiting the witness, where the two defendants were present. They all were sitting around drinking and smoking a blunt, when the female defendant stood up and demanded money from the victim from the victim. The victim did not give the defendant money. The defendant shot the victim one time in the chest. Then she fired one shot into the floor and the gun jammed. The female defendant handed the gun to the male defendant. The female defendant took money and jewelry from the victim as he lay on the floor. The male defendant gave the gun back to the female, they both left together.

The defendant pled guilty to 2nd degree murder and robbery with a dangerous weapon. The defendant was sentence to 162-204 months and 66-89 months consecutive.

When I started working at Women's Prison, I was 26 years old. There were only approximately 450 to 500 inmates, during my career the population grew immensely to 1500 to 1600. There were only 4 to 5 other facilities that we could transfer inmates to, not like the male facilities, which had options to transfer inmates to other facilities because of age, assaultive behavior, maximum, and intensive control. We had inmates that were true maximum control inmates, that you had to keep your eye on when you were dealing with them. We had underage inmates that had to remain in segregation, until they were of age to be released to the grounds, with regular population inmates. We had all custody levels. There was no luxury of sending inmates to another facility like the males. We are a maximum-security prison with a Warden and a Deputy Warden and our pay did not reflect that, this has been a long struggle. The thing now is, we have new Staff coming in making more than someone that has been there for 10 or 15 years, how could this be.

The biggest mistake I feel that could have happen, is when 12 hrs was introduced. I did not care about working 12 hrs. Yes, you worked 14 on and 14 off every other weekend. I will have you to know everything that sound good and always good especially when you had to work your off days. It was both mentally and physically draining. Every other weekend was good and when you took vacation, you could hook your days up, so you could be off for a long period of time. I think originally why we went to 12 hrs was due to shortage of staff and trying to cover the shift in between. I would prefer working two 16 hr days than work 12 hrs. My day would start at 03:45 am. I would have to have time to get up drink my coffee and get myself together. I was not one of those people that could jump up at the last minute, get ready for work and not feel late every time. I would leave home at 05:00 am and get to work at 05:15 or 05:20 am time to change over information, read and adjust my line-up moving staff to man post, robbing Peter to pay Paul and then conduct line up. The day may start fast or slow just be ready. Usually your attitude would determine how your day would be. I would not leave work most of the time until 19:00 pm, some of my staff would not be relieved, because of no relief, the other shift was short of staff. Well by the time they are relieved at 10 or 11, they have worked 16 hrs. Then some of them have to drive an hour to get home turn around and be back at work at 05:45 am. This will take a toll on your body, causing staff to be worn out, irritable, tired and sleepy. Then you have to deal with the inmate 12 more hrs and you are completely worn out. There is a continued concern about the turnover rate. Who wants to work 12 hrs, not this generation out here now! I have had some staff to tell me, I don't have to work, my Mom and Dad will take care of me. When hiring staff don't just give anyone a job. It should be an age limit and more seasoned young adults/adults. BEACON that system should be done away with, because I have always felt that it was taking money from us.

1988

While attending college the defendant convinced to of his friends to help murder his own family, promising to share his inheritance with them if his mother and father were killed. A family owned cleaning chain, estate worth 2 million. The two friends drove to the home and attacked the defendant's mother and father as they slept. The father was stabbed to death, the mother was stabbed and bludgeoned, survived. The defendant's sister was asleep in another part of the house and told police she slept through the whole thing. She was later cleared of any involvement. The defendant remained at the college in order to establish and alibi.

The three were arrested and charged and triad. The defendant whose mother stood by him, admitted being the mastermind of the scheme. The defendant was convicted of aiding and abetting in the assault against his mother and was sentenced to life in prison. The defendant made parole in 2007. The friend was charge with 1st degree murder, eligible for parole in 2022. The other friend was paroled in 2000. This received National attention in role playing games of "Dungeons and Dragons."

2011

A mother and her two teenage children pled guilty to the death of the children's father, who was found decapitated in the freezer of their home. The son was prosecuted as an adult, who was age 13 at the time of the murder.

The father threatens to kill the Mother, a longtime girlfriend, during an argument about the daughter who was 15 at the time. The father stated if the daughter was pregnant, he was going to kill her and bury her in the yard. The daughter was 7 months pregnant. The mother convinced the son to kill his father as he slept. The 13-year-old walked in the room several times with different weapons and told his mother he could not do it. His mother then ordered her son to do it. The teen walked in the room and hit his father in the head twice with a hammer. He did not die immediately. He walked around and crawled around asking for help, the mother refused to help him. He died several hours later, and the family used a dog leash to drag his body to the basement and put him in the freezer. The teen went back to the freezer later and on his own used an ax, knife and a motorized hedge trimmer to decapitate and tried unsuccessfully to cut off his father's legs. He was wrapped in a bed sheet; his head was missing from where it was supposed to be. Even though the mother did not hit the father with the hammer, she was the driving force behind the murder.

She was like a puppet master telling them what to do and they were doing it. She used two teenage children to do what she couldn't do.

2014

The defendant was at a neighbor's residence drinking beer, when the suspect who was a stranger to both of them, approached the victim making a comment and picked up the other individual's beer. When they ask for the beer the suspect became angered. The suspect was then told to leave the property. The suspect had been at the crack house for days getting high and off their medication. Upon the suspect leaving they found a gun lying on the ground. They stated, "I'll blow your fucking brains out." The suspect fired five to six shots towards the house from the street. When the Police arrived, they were still in possession of the gun. The suspect COMPLIED with the officer's orders to drop the gun. The suspect was arrested and charged.

2006

This defendant was convicted of first-degree murder. The victim was at the defendant's residence. The defendant's husband was inside the residence when the defendant came in and informed him that she was going to rob the victim in the front yard because, she needed money and wanted the jewelry they had pawned to victim back. (he owned a pawn shop) the defendant had previously pawned their rings to pay for oxycontin. The defendant's husband told them then that they were crazy and wanted no part of their plan. however, the defendant then got a knife out of a drawer and went back outside. The defendant proceeded to get into an argument with the victim over money that they owed him, and they reached into the victim's pocket and grabbed her ring. The defendant told police that the victim saw their knife and the victim reached under the seat for their gun, and the defendant then stabbed him in the neck. The defendant got in his truck and stabbed the victim some more during the ensuing struggle. The defendant then yelled for the husband to come outside and help. The husband stated, they had seen what happened through a window. The defendant went back inside the house and got a blanket, gave the husband the victim's wallet which contained approximately $5000.00. They both went outside and wrapped up the victim. Then the defendant drove the victim to an old graveyard in the victim's truck followed by the husband in car, dumped the victim out of the car and left to go buy a shovel. They went back and buried the victim about 4 feet in a hole. They then drove down a dirt path and abandoned the truck. The defendant later told police that the victim's truck was set afire. They drove back home. The husband then returned to work that night. The next day the defendant spent approximately $1080.00 on the drug oxycontin. They also bought some clothes and other items with the money. The next day they drove down a road and disposed of the gun and knife in a creek. on 12-15-06, the defendant plead guilty to first degree murder and was given a life sentence. The husband plead guilty to accessory after the fact of first-degree murder, second degree murder, and first-degree kidnapping on 1-25-07.

Working in a prison is like a little small city. It pretty much has all the same attributes of being in the free world, except being free. Inmates have trust fund accounts, 3 meals a day, canteen, medical, dental inside and outside. Once upon a time you could obtain degree, work assignments learn a trade, treatment program for drugs /alcohol, access to telephones, visit with family and children, somewhere to lay their head at night. There are some inmates that find prison as a safe haven, especially, when they have no home or family and living on the streets. As we have to abide by the laws in the free world, inmates have to abide by the rules and the regulations. If you fail to abide by the law you will get picked up by the police and locked up, bond, go to court, get fined or sentenced in prison. If you fail to abide by the rules and regulations in prison you get escorted to lock up 3 days segregation, go to disciplinary get punishment or get fined. In prison when you commit an infraction, you can plead guilty in front of the charging officer and receive punishment or not guilty and be seen by the disciplinary charging Officer. Based on the facts presented it will be determined whether you are guilty or not. I have seen so many teenagers/young adults come into the system and instead of them making the system work for them, while they are incarcerated, they choose to continue the same bad habits that initially brought them to prison. When inmates commit infractions and you have to charge them, you are able to counsel with them and find out what the problem is, an sometimes you can intervene with some of the bad behaviors, most of the time inmates appreciate the fact that you took the time, just to sit down and have a conversation with them and what's going on with them. Then there are some inmates you talk to and your message would pile drive in one ear and do a sprint coming out the other.

There were inmates that seem to be caught in that revolving door as staff always talked about. They just kept coming back and forth to prison with these little crimes that did not carry a lot of time. When they continue to come, they would eventually get hit with a habitual sentence which could be up to 10 yrs.

A lot of times when these inmates are released back out into the society, they are marked with a felony on their record and impossible for them to get a job anywhere except for maybe the fast food chains and gas stations. As you will read throughout the book.

2012

This defendant was reported by loss prevention that the defendant removed inventory control devices and concealed items in their purse. The officer was advised that the defendant left the store without paying for the merchandise, and they confronted and detained them. The Officer found: nine clothing items and one perfume in their purse. Seven of the items had inventory control devices on them and were damaged during removal of the devices. All property that was recovered was about $326 and $281 worth of merchandise was damaged. It was reported that the defendant concealed items, that two other suspects selected. The defendant stated that they were sorry for stealing and know it's wrong but that's how they get money. They stated that they steal for other people and they pay them half price for it. The defendant was banned from the store and charged with larceny. the defendant entered a guilty plea. The defendant was sentenced to 6 yrs. 5 months to 8 yrs. 9 months in prison. however, probation do not recommend early release for the defendant at this time.

2008

Due to the numerous felony forgery and uttering charges. The subject states she and her husband would constantly separate from each other and she would write checks. Each time they separated he would pay off the checks she wrote. The final time they came to prison he refused to pay the checks off. The felony possession of cocaine was the subject states they were on probation at the time and their probation officer came to the house to do a house search. Their daughter's boyfriend was at the house and according to the subject was seen stuffing cocaine in the couch. They claimed when this happened, they were not in the room. However, they were still charged. Their single possession of cocaine offense they pled guilty. Other offenses of forgery and uttering they were placed on probation, which they violated by testing positive for drugs and admitting to illegal drug use.

police investigators reported to a breaking and entering. when they arrived two uniformed officers had two females detained as suspects. The Officers spoke with the neighbors who advised him that the women did not belong there or live there. The witness to the breaking and entering, stated that he saw a black female with a black top being hoisted into the bathroom window of the victim's house. The witness then pointed to one of the females. The bathroom window faces the witnesses house. The female that was lifted up to the window then went in and let the other female in through the front door. At that time the witness called the police. Both suspects were arrested and taken to the station where they were read their rights, and both agreed to be questioned without the presence of a lawyer. Suspect #1 stated that they knew the victim and does tricks for him. They met the other suspect at the house they had just purchased crack from. They stated that the other suspect did not have any money for crack, so they were going to steal something to exchange for crack. They stated they were only going to be the lookout. They also stated that they saw the witness on the phone and figured he was calling the police, so she went in the house to tell suspect #2. Suspect #1 was arrested and was found to be carrying a crack pipe. Suspect #2 stated that the other suspect told them they did tricks for the victim and that he owed them money. Suspect #2 said suspect #1 somehow got into the apartment and let her in the back door. Suspect #2 stated that they were not trying to steal anything and was only there to pool her money with suspect #1 so they could get crack. Both women were transported to the magistrate, where they were charged with breaking and entering.

1989

When a woman was sentenced 28 years ago for the fatal shooting of her husband while he slept in their bed, another woman at the hearing was overwhelmed with emotion. The popular High School football coach found bloodied and near death in his home on Feb. 1, 1988, had confided in his first wife shortly before then that he feared for his safety. He had begun to question whether his wife of seven years, had a hand in her previous husband's death. Had he died in an accidental shooting, as she alleged, or was there something more sinister there – a homicide for which she was never charged?

On February 1st, 1988, the police got a call from a woman, reporting that her husband had been shot. She told the responding officers that her husband kept a handgun under his pillow when he slept, and that she must have touched it as she stirred in her sleep, causing it to discharge and kill her husband. At first the police accepted this account and ruled the incident an accidental shooting. According to shocked friends, coworkers and family members, she was a devoted wife, mother, and Christian.

The first wife is credited with providing continuing evidence of the second wife's spendthrift and adulterous ways as well as the similar death of her first husband. The Attorney was also convinced of her evil nature and piecing together the puzzle and determining that she was guilty of murder. At the conclusion of her trial for first-degree murder on 30 August 1989, the jury deliberated for 44 minutes to reach a guilty verdict, and she was sentenced to death the next day. In such cases the matter is automatically sentence was changed to life imprisonment, due to a technicality in the first proceeding. She was given the possibility of parole in 20 years as required by law.

1991

on Christmas eve of 1990, the defendant was at home with her husband and some friends, who were staying with them temporarily until they could find a place of their own to reside. The defendant and one of the victim's left the house, leaving their husbands, at home drinking that night. The four of them had been partying together and the defendant decided to go to the town to visit one of her friends. While both were in the car, the defendant talked the female into taking her to a friend's house in a rough area of town. The defendant went into the house and stayed longer than expected. The victim told the defendant she was leaving to go back to the house. The victim got in her car, left and returned to the home. When the defendant finally got a ride back to her home, she was very angry and started a fight with the victim for leaving her. The fight became violent and the defendant threatened to stab the victim. The defendant ran into the kitchen, got a butcher knife and came back out into the living room where the victim was. At this point, the victim's husband, the defendant's husband, got in between the two females to try to stop the fight. At that time, the defendant stabbed the male victim in the throat and in the chest. The male victim died from stab wounds to the jugular area of his neck and his upper chest. Alcohol was involved, and drugs were believed to be involved in that the victim had supposedly been using them.

2009

A County jury found a North Carolina woman guilty Thursday of second-degree murder in the stabbing death of a teenager.

The defendant 30, was convicted of killing her victim on May 28, 2004. The jury returned the verdict after deliberating about for four hours.

The Superior Court Judge is expected to sentence the defendant next Friday.

District Attorney told jurors that the defendant killed her victim, who was 19 at the time, out of jealousy. The victim was dating the defendants estranged husband and as a result the defendant had threatened the victim several times and beat her up a week before the murder.

The defendant's husband had walked out on her about five or six months before and had started seeing the victim. During the period between when her husband left her and the murder, the defendant had a lot of animosity toward the victim."

On the day the victim was killed, she and the defendant met up in the parking lot at the old Amoco Gas station. The defendant began a fight by hitting the victim with a beer bottle.

Although the defendant was bigger than the victim, the defendant had been drinking most of the day and the victim was getting the best of her." Then the fight suddenly stopped. The victim stepped back, and everyone realized the defendant had a knife."

The defendant stabbed the victim four times - penetrating her heart and right lung.

The defendant had made the statement that if she couldn't have her husband, nobody could." In the end, the jury found that it wasn't a premeditated killing, but I'm very satisfied with what the jury found."

2001

The defendant committed this crime in 2001, when she killed her boyfriend in which she said he was abusive. The defendant admits to consuming 6 beers prior to the incident, during which she stabbed the victim in the heart and hit the victim in the head with a gun. It happens in her yard at her house. The defendant called 911, stating she had just killed someone. When law enforcement arrived, the defendant was present, and the victim was in the home in a back room lying face down beside the bed. There was a rifle and a gun bloody, sitting in the corner just outside the door. The defendant was searched, and a 6 mm round was found on her person. It appeared she was going to shoot the victim she was arrested at the scene placed in jail and eventually pled guilty to 2nd -degree murder. The defendant was sentenced to a 180 month and a maximum term of 225 months in prison.

1998

The defendant stated that her son had come over to visit, she asks him to leave before her husband the son's (stepfather) woke up. The defendant stated that the son shoved her against the wall and woke up her husband. The defendant stated she was trying to pick herself up off the floor when the husband came through the door with a knife and stabbed the victim in the back. The defendant stated that the victim was able to get out the house and collapsed in a neighbor's yard. The eldest son had reported his suspicions. The defendant stated although her husband had testified against her that she was in fact involved in plotting her son's murder.

The court determined that these to defendant conspires to kill the victim, to get him out the way and collect his insurance benefits. The defendant was convicted of 1st-degree murder and conspiracy to commit murder. The defendant was sentenced to Life in prison.

1986

Officers of the Wilmington Police Department responded to a telephone call from 19-year-old defendant stating that she had found her mother dead in an upstairs closet of her apartment. Upon arrival, the police discovered the badly decomposing body of the 36-year-old victim. The body was transferred that same day, where Assistant Chief Medical Examiner performed an autopsy. The autopsy revealed that the cause of death was suffocation.

The victim and two of her children, age 17; a cousin age 19; and a friend, age 19, two-year old child, two-month old infant and one-year old baby were also residing in the apartment.

The cousin went to the police station and informed the police that the daughter had murdered her mother on. The cousin admitted her involvement in the case and turned state's witness. The two defendants also agreed to testify for the state against defendant in return for lesser charges being filed against them. In the next two days, defendant was arrested and indicted for murder in the first degree and conspiracy.

At trial, the sister recalled that on the morning her sister woke her up saying "Let's get mama." They went downstairs and found the victim lying on the couch with her face to the wall. She was listening to the stereo. Defendant deliberately turned the stereo off and the television on. The victim said she wanted to listen to the stereo and cut the television off. This happened several times and victim finally said, "If that's going to make you feel any better, you can leave it on." Defendant replied, "No, it won't make me feel any better until you fight me like you wanted to fight me last night." Finally, the victim sat back down because "she really didn't want to argue with the daughter " the Defendant then called the other three defendants into the kitchen and asked them to help her hit her mother in the head with a Pepsi-Cola bottle. All three of the girls refused because they were afraid. Defendant asserted, "I'm not scared, I'll hit her in the head with the bottle." Defendant returned to the room where her mother was resting, renewed the argument and hit her mother in the head with the bottle. The victim yelled, "That's enough, I'm going to call the cops. You're going to jail now." As she turned to go to the telephone, she tripped over the coffee table and fell. Defendant immediately sat on her chest to hold her down and began choking her with her hands. At some point, the victim called out to one of the defendants that "if you'll help me, I'll give you a hundred dollars." Defendant asked her sister to hand her the pillow which she had specially prepared by wrapping it in plastic bags and placed on the stairs. The defendant did so and held it over her mother's face for "more than ten minutes." The victim struggled for approximately three to five minutes. Defendant then announced, "Mama's dead." At some point, defendant made the other girls touch the pillow so that they would all be involved in the murder. The cousin and the friend assisted the daughter in carrying the body upstairs where it was placed into the hall closet and covered with sheets and clothes.

Approximately two weeks prior to the murder, one of the defendant's recalled going to the bank with defendant to withdraw money from her account. Upon finding that the account was empty, defendant said, "I'm going to get her." The defendant testified that on that very night defendant had a pillow and said she was going to use it to get her mother. Apparently, defendant "chickened out and said she couldn't do it."

At some point prior to her death, the victim, had been diagnosed as suffering from a paranoid schizophrenic disorder and had been involuntarily committed for psychiatric treatment an undetermined number of times. As a result, she was unable to perform her job duties at Textiles and began receiving social security benefits. Because of her particular disability, it was determined that victim was incapable of handling her own business affairs. Therefore, the defendant, the oldest child living in the same household, was named as payee. Three days before her death, the victim went to the local Social Security office and spoke with a claim's representative. According to them, the victim suspected her oldest daughter of spending the checks and wished to change her named payee. The representative called the daughter to inform her of her mother's wishes and to ask her the whereabouts of a retroactive disability check in the amount of $5,395.00. When defendant stated that she still held the check, the representative asked her to return it as soon as possible. The check was not returned.

The cousin testified that one or two nights before the victim's death, defendant had attempted to suffocate her mother but decided against it when she realized her face was turned to the wall. The friend also gave evidence of several occasions upon which defendant had obtained various types of pills to put into her mother's beer or water for the purpose of putting her to sleep. On the evening before the murder, "[s]he was upstairs in her room, she already had it mixed and she was shaking the bottle."

Defendant did not testify and presented no evidence.

The jury found defendant guilty of first-degree murder and conspiracy. At the conclusion of the penalty phase of the trial, the jury unanimously recommended that defendant be sentenced to life imprisonment on the murder conviction. Accordingly, the trial judge sentenced defendant to life imprisonment on the first-degree murder conviction and imposed a ten-year sentence on the conspiracy conviction.

2006 SCHOOL SHOOTING

On August 2006, former student 18-year-old murdered his father and then drove the family minivan to the High School, where he set off a Cherry Bomb and then opened fire with a <u>9mm</u> <u>Hi-Point 995 Carbine</u> and a <u>sawed-off</u> <u>12-gauge Mossberg 500</u> <u>pump-action shotgun</u>. When his carbine jammed, he was apprehended by a deputy sheriff assigned to the school and a retired highway patrol officer who taught driver's education. Two students were injured in the attack, but none were killed.

Later that day it was discovered that the 18-year-old had killed his father to "put him out of his misery." He also made the statement of another horrific school shooting in another state while entering a patrol car, referring to the high school shooting in 1999. He sent a written letter and videotape to the News prior to the shooting, that made reference to the school shooting. He also sent an e-mail to the principal of that high school saying "Dear Principal, in a few hours you will probably hear about a school shooting in North Carolina. I am responsible for it. I remember. It is time the world remembered it. I am sorry. Goodbye."

He entered a plea of not guilty by reason of insanity Psychologist testified that the 18 year old suffered from <u>schizotypal</u> and <u>obsessive-compulsive personality disorder,</u> as well as <u>major depressive disorder</u> and was not in touch with reality at the time of the shooting. On August 2009, he was found guilty in County Superior Court following a trial that lasted three weeks. He was sentenced to life in prison with no chance of parole.

As a supervisor coming through the rank, I felt when you move up things were supposed to slow down or become less stressful. It would be more about supervising staff and being an OIC Officer in Charge, instead of the Officer, Sergeant, Unit Manager, Lieutenant and the damn Captain. If you can work at women's prison, you can work at any prison. I really don't think that other prisons did all of what we done. It was great learning experience though, but there were moments you were just damn tired. Working at women's prison made you have knowledge and knowledge was power. Only the strong can survive. There would be staff that would leave our facility and go to another. They would say that other prisons don't do what y'all do. Staff going to other facilities would see that the grass was not always greener on the other side of the fence. It is not the bars or stripes that make you. It's about trust, respect, knowledge and integrity, which give you the means to have power, to do the thing that need to be done. You had to make decisions and be able to stand by them at a minute notice and not have to call someone to have them to make the decision for you, because you don't want to be held accountable. There was certain thing you should have master by time you became a Captain. Communication and people skills are the key. Sometimes you had to take the bitter with the salt; bitter with the sweet is to easy. I loved what I did and did what I loved.

Communicating with the inmate population was what I loved. That's how you learn about the inmate and their way of living, finding out what's going on, on the compound, in the dormitories and the work projects, most of the time, if there was anything about to happen, you would have time to intervene, if you needed to. I would go out on the yard and sit and talk with the inmates. Sometimes I would just stand in a particular place, just so I could be seen by most. The inmates that did not see me, would get word from their buddies, that I was out on the yard. The inmates would see me and ask "why was I on the yard? You looking for somebody." I would say no; can't I be out on the yard if I want to?" This inmate was probably a lookout person for other inmates, that were committing infractions. Women always have something to talk about staff and inmates, most of the time if you talk to them; it keeps down a lot of confusion. Some inmates play the game of asking one staff something and when they don't get the answer they want, they will go to the next staff person, until they get what they want, just like children.

We have many staff becoming undue with inmates, but it wouldn't last for long, because soon as that inmate get mad about something, they going to tell on you and all the staff they have information on, to use as leverage. Staff being undue whether it was having sex, being in a relationship was not an option. I think some of the people that were hired already knew or was an associate of the inmate prior to applying for the job.

ANSON COUNTY, N.C. — A prison guard is going to prison for making deals with inmates she was supposed to be overseeing.

Channel 9 reporter was in the courtroom when the judge decided to give the Correctional Officer, who used to work at Correctional Institute, the toughest punishment, sentencing her to a year and a half in federal prison.

The Correctional Facility is one of the most dangerous prisons in North Carolina where there have been assaults, stabbings and murder, and it's generally believed that the gangs, not the guards, run the place.

The Correctional Facility was one of the most difficult problems that former FBI Assistant Director dealt with when he was the chairman of the governor's crime commission.

He said corruption is rampant.

"It's an extremely difficult situation for someone who is not willing to be compromised. Reports said she was introduced to a high-ranking gang member by another guard.

She then took money in exchange for giving contraband, like tobacco, pot and phones to the inmates.

"Staff are there with them for long stretches of time and so you build relationships and those relationships can sometimes be exploited," said a professor at UNC Charlotte.

The professor doesn't see the situation turning around at the correctional Facility without some major help.

"No routine effort will fix what's wrong with these types of prisons in North Carolina; there has to be a major overhaul." It will cost a lot of money to fix the problem. The Professor believes a good start would be to raise salaries and fully staff the facility.

Nine people, including a Department of Public Safety correctional officer, are facing charges in a prison drug-distribution ring throughout North Carolina, officials said, WTVD reported. The ringleader of a distribution network of Suboxone that stretched across North Carolina state prisons. The Suboxone went from an Urgent Care through the network and into the prisons, according to authorities. "This type of criminal activity is a slap in the face to the hardworking, underpaid employees of the NC Department of Corrections who keep our communities safe from those who choose to commit serious crimes in our great state," said the County Sheriff. The individual who worked as a correctional officer at the women's prison in Raleigh, was accused of conspiring with the ringleader to deliver Suboxone and was charged with felony conspiracy to sell and deliver a Schedule III narcotic.

Sergeant at another Correctional Institution in North Carolina has been arrested for trying to bring drugs into the prison. One of the most dangerous prison correctional Facilities in North Carolina.

The Sergeant, 34, was arrested by the Police Department after an internal investigation into her alleged conduct. The sergeant was arrested at work while on duty. She resigned her position effective immediately following the arrest.

The Sergeant was specifically charged with Felony Conspiracy to Deliver Marijuana and Suboxone to an Inmate and Felony Possession of Marijuana and Suboxone.

Suboxone is used to reduce symptoms of opiate addiction and withdrawal.

The inmates would seek out new staff that seem weak or timid. Nothing good will ever come out of this. That would be the game of certain, inmates to pick staff out. Don't look for love and friendship in the wrong place. Inmates know all the right things to say to get your attention. They tell you how nice you look, and you smell good, to strike up that conversation with you. Next thing you know they are looking for you when you come to work and will take a write up to see you or come to your post.

1974

Nearly three months later, before dawn on August 27, 1974, a police officer delivering a drunken prisoner to the County jail discovered the body of jailer 62, on defendant's bunk, naked from the waist down. He had suffered stab wounds to the temple and the heart area from an icepick. Semen was discovered on his leg. The defendant was missing. She turned herself in to North Carolina authorities more than one week later, and said that she had killed the jailer while defending herself against sexual assault.

The victim had a record of forcing female inmates to take part in sexual favors as payment for gifts he'd give the inmates earlier. Other inmates had come forward and stated that he had given them gifts in the form of snacks and magazines and expected to receive sexual favors.

Since the defendant had fled from prison she was known as a fugitive and the ability to kill her on sight was targeted on her, due to this the defendant turned herself in. The defendant was on trial for murder and was facing the gas chamber. The defendant had found refuge in the home of an older black man from her community as well as had received offers to seek refuge in other countries.

98 percent of staff-on-inmate sexual assault is male staff against female inmates.

Charged with first degree murder

She was charged with first degree murder, which carried an automatic death sentence. The capital status of the case, and the fact that North Carolina was home to over one third of all the death penalty cases in the United States, drew the attention of anti-death penalty and prisoners' rights advocates. During the time of the defendant's trial there were two other women of color facing the death penalty. The defendant's trial brought attention to her being the first women of color to cite self-defense during sexual assault against an accusation of murder. The racial component drew the attention of civil rights activists, and the gender component drew the attention of feminists. The combination of these three factors, along with sophisticated fundraising tactics, allowed the Defense Committee to raise over $350,000. The question of whether or not blacks were treated equally by the criminal justice systems in the American South drew the attention of the national media.

Women on death row

From 1973 to the end of 2017, 184 women have been sentenced to death row in the United States. Sixteen were sentenced to death in North Carolina, with only three still remaining on death row since 2013. From 1976 to 2016 sixteen women have been executed for murder. Since the 1900s 54 women have been executed. Out of 165 inmates exonerated since March 2019, only two were females.

At trial, the prosecution contended that the defendant was a lewd woman who seduced the victim only to murder him to enable her escape. In two days of testimony, the defendant testified that victim, who at well over 200 pounds was nearly twice her size, had come to her cell three times between 10:00 pm and 3:00 am to solicit sex, finally forcing her at the point of an ice pick to perform oral sex. She testified she was able to seize the ice pick while he was seated on her bunk because he had let his guard down in the moments after his orgasm. She stabbed him repeatedly, and she testified he resisted fiercely and wrestled her, but that given his wounded state, she had been able to get free of him. The Attorney made liberal use of the jury's Southern Christian sympathies, characterizing his client as a religious woman who found solace in the Bible in times of trouble.

The prosecutor had concluded that the defendant had lured the 62-year-old jailer, so she could escape.

When the autopsy came back, it was concluded that the explanation of the incident was true. The autopsy concluded that the eleven stab wounds given to the victim were in self-defense. Only one stab had been a fatal one, while the other ten were clear signs of self-defense against an attacker.

The jury of six whites and six African Americans deliberated for one hour and 25 minutes and rendered a verdict of not guilty.

The defendant walked around in front of publicity with the book "To Kill a Mockingbird".

The Free the defendant's campaigns were successful enough that the defendant's counsel was able to get the first-degree murder charge reduced to second degree. The Judge noted that the prosecution did not have liable evidence.

The defendant was returned to prison to serve the remainder of her sentence for breaking and entering. One month before she would have been eligible for parole, she made an escape. She was caught and then convicted and sentenced for the escape. She was freed in June 1979 and moved to New York City

RALEIGH (WTVD) -- Investigators have charged 32-year-old former Correctional Officer with having sex with inmates at Raleigh's women's prison.

The Officer was fired when the investigators first began looking into the allegations last year.

According to the affidavit of an investigator's search warrant obtained by ABC11, the investigation began in August after the bureau was asked to look into "An allegation from female inmates that indicated that these individuals had consensual sex with a correctional officer." Consensual sex with prisoners is illegal in North Carolina.

The search warrant was for the Officer's DNA, which investigators said they wanted to use to compare with any DNA found on the clothing of female inmates at the Prison.

State officials say they were given a positive employment reference from another state on the Officer even though he resigned because of "a substantiated allegation of... having a sexual relationship with a female inmate" in that state.

The Officer is accused of having sex with four inmates between June 1, 2015 and Aug. 18, 2015. One of these inmates was convicted in a high-profile quadruple murder case in 2003. She was only convicted of three of those murders and is serving life without parole.

ASHEVILLE - Buncombe County sheriff's deputies arrested a North Carolina Department of Public Safety correctional sergeant who is accused of having sex with an inmate at Correctional Center for Women, where he is employed, according to warrants.

The sergeant, 44, of has been charged with six felony counts of sex acts by a government employee.

He is on paid leave for unrelated reasons, NCDPS spokesman told the Citizen Times. He could not say whether the sergeant would be suspended when he returns, citing a plethora of factors that would need to be considered.

"We take these issues very seriously. This is under criminal investigation; the Department of Public Safety is cooperating fully with that investigation."

The sergeant was originally hired as a correctional officer in January 2005 and was promoted to his current position in 2012.

The dates of his alleged offenses were between Sept. 1 and Oct. 7, according to warrants.

The sergeant received an unsecured bond of $50,000 and was not listed as an inmate in the Buncombe County jail's digital database on Nov. 25. He was scheduled to appear in court that day.

CHARLOTTE, N.C. – A federal grand jury sitting in Charlotte has indicted Correctional Officer 46, for smuggling a controlled substance at a Correctional Institution while employed as a correctional officer. The indictment was unsealed today in federal court, following the Officer's arrest by the FBI.

According to charges contained in the federal indictment, He worked as a correctional officer at the Correctional Institution, since renamed as another state prison located in North Carolina.

According to the indictment, between August and September 2018, while employed at the facility as a correctional officer, he accepted a bribe to smuggle a controlled substance into the facility on behalf of an inmate housed at the facility. *The Officer is charged with use of interstate facility to facilitate bribery, which carries a maximum prison term of five years and a $250,000 fine; extortion under color of official right, which carries a maximum prison term of 20 years and a $250,000 fine; and possession with intent to distribute a controlled substance, which carries a maximum prison term of 10 years and a $250,000 fine.*

RALEIGH - United States Attorney announces that on August 19, 2015, a federal grand jury in Raleigh returned a four count Indictment against two former Correctional Officers that worked at the Correctional Institution in Butner, North Carolina.

The Indictment charges each with one count of Extortion Under Color of Official Right. Additionally, one was charged with one count of making a False Statement to the Federal Bureau of Investigation, and one count of lying before a federal Grand Jury. U.S. Attorney stated, "Corruption by correction officers undermines the criminal justice system and puts the general public at risk. We will always prosecute these kinds of cases to maintain the integrity of our system."

One Ex Officer was employed as a Correctional Officer at the Correctional Facility from 2005, through May of 2015. From 2012, through September of 2014, they held the position of Sergeant and worked as a supervisor in the facility's "high security maximum control unit." The unit was opened in 1998 to serve as North Carolina's supermax prison for "the state's most violent and assaultive offenders." The indictment alleges that the Ex Correctional Officer engaged in a scheme with several prisoners held in the facility under which he smuggled tobacco, marijuana, cellular telephones, and packages of AA batteries (often used to fashion a device for charging the cellular telephones) to such inmates in exchange for cash. The cellular telephones were used by the inmates to communicate with persons outside of prison. It is further alleged that, after being transferred out of the unit in September of 2014, he continued to smuggle contraband into the facility for at least one additional inmate.

The other Ex C/O is alleged to have misused his position as a Correction Officer to extort things of value from inmates. He is also alleged to have lied as to a material fact during an interview with FBI Agents and to have committed perjury while testifying before a federal Grand Jury.

The United States Attorney's Office and FBI's investigation into the facility was prompted by the circumstances relating to the kidnapping conspiracy alleged to have been orchestrated by a defendant through the use of a cellular telephone in his cell.

"These men put many lives at risk for their own profit. They were entrusted with the responsibility of ensuring that North Carolina's convicted criminals serve their sentences. Instead, this type of conduct made it possible for a dangerous inmate to reach outside of prison walls which lead to the kidnapping. The FBI will keep pursuing this case and will not stop until everyone who played a role in this ruthless crime is held accountable," said Special Agent in Charge of the FBI.

The facility is operated under the purview of the North Carolina Department of Public Safety. "The department has participated in and cooperated with this investigation and we strongly support this prosecution in this very serious case to the fullest extent of the law. DPS has so many professional and dedicated employees who serve the state in this very challenging and dangerous environment and it is truly regrettable when a corrupt staff member puts their co-workers and the public at risk."

If convicted of Extortion Under Color of Official Rights both defendants face maximum imprisonment of 20 years and a fine of $250,000. In addition, faces a maximum of 5 years imprisonment if convicted of making a False Statement and a fine of $250,000- and 5-years imprisonment if convicted of Perjury and a fine of $250,000.

The charges and allegations contained in the Indictment are merely accusations. The defendants are considered innocent unless and until proven guilty in a court of law.

The case is being investigated by the Federal Bureau of Investigation and prosecuted by Assistant U.S. Attorneys.

Correctional employees and inmates can also be the targets of assaults, when inmates feel they have been abused or mistreated. Your actions, being disrespectful of them and their belongings or other inmates. The old saying is "be careful of how you treat people."

So, guess what People? as my Mom can say "everything that look good ain't good, never judge a book by its cover." This type of so-called staff can and will be working with you or near you and some of you would never know.

The inmates always knew what was going on, a lot of them would turn their heads to the fact, saying they don't wanna get involved or be labeled a snitch. There were inmates that would sit and watch everything, they would know when something was going to go down. They have already heard it through inmate. com. Women we like to talk, so if something was about to happen you will have a two-week head start on trying to intervene.

Cellphones, drugs, chargers and cigarettes were stuffed into footballs hurled over the prison-wire fence, but the pass was intercepted.

Contraband — meant for inmates at the Correctional Institution — never made it past the defense of a vigilant employee at the prison's meat processing plant.

The Corrections Enterprises worker saw someone outside the perimeter, tossing something over the fence on according to the state communications officer of adult corrections. When staff members went to investigate, they found 11 footballs, which had been cut open, filled with the contraband and taped shut. The items were seized by prison staff.

"I have to commend our staff for the outstanding job they do on a daily basis here," said the Warden. "Their training and experience in curtailing contraband keeps everyone safe."

The footballs contained a treasure trove of illicit items: 11 cellphones, about a pound of loose tobacco, 283 cigarettes, a dozen phone chargers, a Bluetooth speaker, a beard trimmer, two watches, 50 grams of the synthetic marijuana K2 (Spice),

four bottles of liquid K2, two grams of marijuana and a pack of rolling papers.

North Carolina Commissioner of Prisons, said the attempt to send the items into the facility and the subsequent seizure, was just another challenge to staff who are charged with maintaining security at the prison.

"Contraband remains a challenge in prisons, even during a pandemic, "It's remarkable. But our staff is remarkable as well. They do a great job."

RALEIGH, N.C. (WNCN) — The Department of Public Safety said one of its workers has been charged with misdemeanor secret peeping. The employee is accused of taking a video camera into a restroom at the Correctional Facility.

The employee told CBS 17 it was a prank. He said the camera wasn't operational and that the whole thing was blown out of proportion. He declined a request for an interview.

According to the arrest warrant, the restroom was used by an inmate and staff.

DPS said he is an employee and that he works as an electronics technician. He's held that position since 2011.

He was most recently assigned to another institution.

"The Department of Public Safety has zero tolerance for any staff involved in any illegal activity," a statement said. "The

Department has many hard-working correctional professionals and it takes staff arrests very seriously. The Department is fully cooperating with law enforcement."

This was before my time, but a lot of the public is unaware of.

Prison and Execution Wikipedia

There was an American serial killer who was convicted of one murder, but who eventually confessed to six murders in total. This defendant was the first woman in the United States to be executed after the 1976 resumption of capital punishment and the first since 1962. She was also the first woman to be executed by lethal injection.

Born in rural county, her father reportedly was physically abusive and her mother, did not intervene. She escaped by getting married. The couple had two children and were reportedly happy until she had surgery and developed back pain. These events led to a behavioral change in her and an eventual drug addiction.

The husband began to drink, and her complaints turned into bitter arguments. After he had passed out, she and the children left the house, and when they returned, they found the structure burned and he was dead. A few months later, her own home burned down but was insured, she married a widower. Less than a year after their marriage, he died from heart complications.

Her mother, showed symptoms of intense diarrhea, vomiting and nausea, only to fully recover a few days later. During the Christmas season of the same year, the mother experienced the same earlier illness, but died in the hospital a few hours after being admitted.

The defendant began caring for the elderly, working for a couple. When one of the victims fell ill and died. A little over a month after the death of the husband, the wife experienced identical symptoms and died. The defendant later confessed to the latter death. The following year, she took another caretaker job, this time for 76-year-old, who had broken his leg. The victim's husband, began experiencing racking pains in his stomach and chest along with vomiting and diarrhea. He died soon afterward, and the defendant later confessed to his murder.

Another victim was the defendant's boyfriend and a relative of the other victims. Fearing he had discovered she had been forging checks on his account, she mixed an arsenic-based rat poison into his beer and tea. He died, while she was trying to "nurse" him back to health; an autopsy found arsenic in his system. After her arrest, the body of the victim was exhumed and found to have traces of arsenic, a murder that she denied having committed. Although she subsequently confessed to the murders of the other victims, she was tried and convicted only for the murder of the boyfriend.

Singer-songwriter was the grandson of the victim and his first wife. His song from his album gives a personal account of the murders and investigation.

After the defendant's appeal was denied in federal court, she instructed her attorneys to abandon a further appeal to the U.S. Supreme Court. The defendant was executed on November 2, 1984. She released a statement before the execution: "I know that everybody has gone through a lot of pain, all the families connected, and I am sorry, and I want to thank everybody who have been supporting me all these six years. She chose her last meal 1 bag of Cheetos and two 8-ounce glass bottles of Coca-Cola. The defendant was buried in the small rural county cemetery near her first husband.

2001

The victim had just returned from picking up a carry out food order. The victim was expecting his girlfriend to stop by. The victim went to answer the knock at the door, shortly after their return. The victim asks, "who is it" After looking through the peep hole. The victim stated "I can't see you" to whomever was outside the door. The victim still expecting his girlfriend, the victim opened the door. As the door was being opened, the victim saw a silver handgun described as a large revolver come through the door opening. The gun starts firing. It continued to fire until it started clicking, which the victim thought it was empty. Both victims then tried to close the door. The victim's continued to try and close the door, but the shooter's arm and part of their body prevented the door from closing. After securing the door one victim was grazed in the leg, one in the stomach and the other victim in the side who later died. The suspect had been identified from a photo lineup.

2001

The defendant called 911 and stated she had been shot. The authorities found the defendant with her husband and the children in the home. The defendant's husband was dead. The defendant was taken to the hospital, where she was questioned by Law enforcement. Questioning by the authorities lead them to assume that the defendant murdered her husband with the help of an accomplice. The defendant arrives a few days prior to the murder. The accomplice slept in the back yard of the defendant, until the night of the murder. The other defendant came into the home, as the defendant and her husband sleep. The defendant woke up once she heard the other defendant inside. The gun was pulled on the victim while he was asleep. The defendants blame each other. The defendant stated he could not see the defendant hurt. They should make it look a break in and an attack on her, to make it look like a robbery gone bad. The defendant was convicted of 2nd degree murder and conspiracy to commit murder.

Working in lock up and there was a code called, you be like where did all this staff come from. You never knew the circumstances and because there have been so many times that staff has been assaulted.

Inmate Assault on Staff: On March 25, DPS officials announced that attempted murder charges were being filed against an offender who assaulted correctional officer at a Correctional Institution with a homemade weapon on March 19.The inmate age 47, was charged by the Police Department with attempted murder, assault with a deadly weapon against a government official, and possession of a weapon by a prisoner. He is scheduled to appear in County Court on the charges. The Correctional Officer a 17-year-veteran, was attacked in a housing dorm at approximately 10:05 a.m. The Officer was treated for her wounds and discharged from the hospital later that day, at approximately 9:30 p.m. The inmate was removed from the facility and remains in restrictive housing at a Maximum Correctional Institution in Butner. The inmate was serving a 49-year sentence for first degree rape and was admitted to prison on Feb. 4, 1998.

WINDSOR, N.C. (AP) — A state official confirms three correctional officers were assaulted at the North Carolina prison where staff was killed two years ago.

WITN reports the state Department of Public Safety says an inmate at Correctional Institution hit a sergeant and two officers last Friday afternoon.

A DPS spokesman says no serious injuries were reported and the officers were able to subdue the inmate.

In April 2017, A Sergeant. was beaten to death with a fire extinguisher at the Correctional Facility.

A lawsuit by the Sergeant's father contends prison officials didn't respond when convicted killer said he needed psychological help to combat homicidal thoughts before he killed the Correctional Sergeant. Prosecutors are seeking the death penalty.

Elizabeth City 2017 Four correctional staff were killed during an attempted escape attempt from a correctional facility.

2017 was the most horrific year I've ever known for staff, in the state of North Carolina. You always have to remain vigilant watching different signs and behaviors of the inmate population. Don't become comfortable and let your guard down.

You just didn't know! Working in Eagle housing (lock up) there was never a boring minute. Disciplinary Hearing would be held in this area, to keep from bringing inmates out of the segregation area. There would be a classification committee that would come and make decisions of whether an inmate would remain on segregation. I had brought in an inmate who had assaultive behavior, to talk with the committee, she was calm for the most part. When I brought her out the cell and escorted her to the conference room, where the classification committee was, that usually consisted of 2 males. I escorted her in the room the inmate sits down. The committee talked with her for a few minutes and then asks her to step out, while they deliberated whether or not the inmate would remain on the present control or be taken off. When we returned the committee gave their decision, which the inmate did not like, before I knew anything this inmate had turned around pulled her dress up and mooned the committee. LOL the males were like Oh My Lord! With their hands, up to their faces. I immediately removed the inmate from the immediate area. There was an inmate that was being escorted from point A to point B. Upon the staff exiting with the inmate, the inmate took off running around the building fully restrained. This was a very dangerous position that this inmate had put their self in, playing games with the Sgt that was escorting them.

We as correctional staff must stay vigilant always of what is going on around us being observant, listen and report anything out the ordinary (RED FLAGS). If you feel it, or you think it. It probably is don't underestimate. Remember it is always your DUTY TO REPORT!! Whether it is staff or inmates.

2008

The defendant called a friend stated he wanted to rob someone. The defendant drove to the area and searched for a victim. Once they located their victim, they were forced into the backseat of the car and held hostage with a gun to the victim's head. The victim was carried to several ATM's where they rob them of $700.00. the victim tried to reason with them, begging for their life. Telling them they could take whatever they wanted, and they did not need to kill them, because the victim had seen their faces, the defendant's decided to kill their victim. Blood found in the victim's lungs indicated they were still alive and breathing after being shot with a handgun. The fifth and fatal shot she suffered was from a sawed off 12-gauge shotgun. Both defendants were apprehended. Later charged with first degree murder, armed robbery and kidnapping. They were found guilty and sentenced to Life in prison without the possibility of parole.

Police received and responded to a 911 call concerning shots fired in the area. Officers were told by the callers that they heard a gunshot and a scream and 3 more shots. As Officers patrolled the area, they observed something lying in the roadway. As the officer's got closer, it was determined that the object was a person. Once the Officer's got out their vehicle, it was called in a body of a female suffering from a gunshot wound to the right side of the head. No ID was on the body. The body had suffered4 handgun wounds and 2 shotgun wounds. The wound to the right temporal caused the death of the victim.

2001

A 17-year-old girl and her 20-year-old boyfriend have been charged with murdering the girl's mother and dumping her body in an isolated area near Lake.

The two defendants were charged with murder Saturday in the death of 46-year-old according to the County Sheriff's Department. The two were being held Sunday in the County Jail with no bond. A first court appearance was set for today. Sheriff's deputies from the County were called to the area near a Lake after passers-by discovered the body about 3:20 p.m. Saturday. Investigators discovered what county that the body was in and deputies from that county took over the investigation. In contrast to defendants' statements, the other defendant testified in Sept. 2001 that it was the daughter's idea to kill her mother and that the two planned an ambush together in advance before he ultimately carried out the actions.

The daughter pleaded not guilty and was found guilty of first-degree murder on Sept. 28, 2001. She was sentenced to life in prison without parole. However, according to an N.C. Court of Appeals decision in 2003, The defendant was given a new trial and found guilty in 2005 of aiding and abetting second-degree murder and accessory after the fact to first-degree murder. She was sentenced to 131 to 167 months in prison.

The defendant now 34, was released from the prison on Jan. 2 after serving 12 years and 11 months for aiding and abetting second-degree murder and accessory after the fact to first-degree murder. That sentence came after a successful appeal of her earlier conviction which would have put her behind bars for life.

2005

The defendant states they had been dating the victim for about 3 months and they had been fighting for about 2 days. They both had been drinking too much. While at the victim's house. The victim was sitting on the passenger side of the van and the defendant got into the van and they talked with each other for a while. They both were angry and at some point, they both got out the van. He had a gun in his waist band when he got out. He put the gun in the door pocket on the passenger side. The defendant has seen him carry a gun before, but he did not point it at her or threaten her with it. They got out the van and continued to argue. At some point he grabbed the defendant breast and twisted, it hurt the defendant bad. The defendant got real mad grabbed the gun from the truck. The defendant was mad that the victim grabbed her breast like that, and she just pointed the gun at his head and shot the victim.

We would have inmates that were very assaultive, and you would have to proceed with caution. These inmates were locked down 23 hrs a day 7 days a week. They had 1 hour out of their cell 15 mins for shower and 45 mins to exercise. We would have inmates get in the shower and refuse to get out, because they didn't want to go back to their cell, so here we are trying to talk to the inmate and get them back in their cell. Sometimes talking worked and sometimes it did not. If we had to remove inmate from the shower, they will be wet and soaped down which made it difficult. These inmates would be on all types of medication, to keep them calm, if they miss a dose staff would be in for a rude awakening. We would have to go up against what seemed like 10 men, which usually resulted in staff getting assaulted or hurt and then they would have to be out of work or on some type of an accommodation, there again causing a shortage of staff. Once there was an inmate brought in underage, she was a lot of mouth from what I could see doing a lot of cursing and calling names and she probably was just scared trying to make other inmates think she was bad. I happen to be with the disciplinary committee this particular day. So, the Capt at the time went to assist other staff with this inmate. I heard a lot of commotion going on down on the block. I left disciplinary hearing and proceeded to the block where I saw the Capt. I immediately told the Capt to step back, because I didn't want them to get hurt. The Capt said the same to me. I assist staff with placing this inmate in the cell, as the inmate refused, me being who I was faced off with this inmate and ask her what her problem was, she continued cursing and name calling. We began to exit the cell and the inmate became confident to buck against us. This inmate was primarily putting on a show for the other inmates housed on that block, to let them see she was bad, and they better not mess with her.

These inmates received their breakfast, lunch and dinner meals in their cells. The food carts would be brought by the dining room workers and the staff would distribute them. This was another way for inmate to get contraband into these lock- up areas, hiding items in the food trays, food or even on the cart. If staff distributing the trays did not check them thoroughly, inmates would get in any and all contraband. Inmates would be escorted outside 45 mins for exercise. When the weather was inclement, provided it was enough staff, the inmate would exercise on their blocks one at a time. Staff would gather the inmate's canteen list for them, to purchase items from the canteen. You would have inmates that were on restricted privileges through the disciplinary process. The one thing they hated most, was to have the canteen restricted, whether it was no canteen or only drawing $10.00 a month. They would only be allowed to purchased hygiene items. Most of the inmates in lock up were the ones that could not follow the rules and regulations and was receiving write ups back to back or had several write ups. They just couldn't follow the rules. There was one time an inmate had grown a full beard/mustache and looked just like a dude, they were only allowed to shave every so often because they were a self-mutilator. Staff would have to monitor them utilizing a razor. Even then somehow whenever they could use the razor, it would end up being a horrific day for staff in that area. This inmate along with another inmate, who also was a self-mutilator were supposedly in love with one another. They had to be kept separated on different blocks. If one was causing disruption and confusion, then the other one would to. (two peas in a pot) A lot of time inmates would do just enough to seek attention for someone anyone (cry Wolfe). Then inmates would do things that cause serious injury to themselves, like cut a major artery and have blood spewing out everywhere. Working with staff from other facilities, they would tell their horror stories about inmates. One-time inmate cut their stomach with a razor, causing their intestine, to be exposed as they were in their arm-hand. I could only imagine seeing that.

2002

on September 21, 2002 the body of a victim was discovered. The police received information that the victim was meeting (his step-granddaughter) on the night of September 20, 2002. The meeting was for purposes of a proposed monetary settlement between the victim and the granddaughter for past grievances she had with him. Agents and several deputies went to the home on the night of September 21, 2002 looking for her after the discovery of the victims badly beaten body. When they did not find her, they left info with friends and relatives directing them to have the defendant contact the police when she got back into town. What the police did not know at this time was that the defendant and her boyfriend had gone to the beach for a weekend of drinking and drug use after murdering victim with a baseball bat. The two arrived back in town on the afternoon of September 22, she was told by several people that she needed to call an agent about the death of her step-grandfather. She spoke with the agent and arranged for them to meet at the police department. Shortly after she spoke with the agent, the deputy and the county sheriff arrived at the residence finding that the defendants were at the residence. At the time, there was a bolo (be-on-the-lookout). The approached the residence with his shotgun in his arms. He placed the defendants in handcuffs and placed them in his car. The agent then proceeded to search mote's truck that was parked at the residence discovering a baseball bat and some knives. The agent subsequently called the sheriff's department and discovered that the defendants were expected at the police station. The agent then released the defendants but told them if they did not go to the police station, he would be back to get them. The female defendant went to the police station. She was led to an investigation room with detective and agents. During the interrogation, the defendant made incriminating statements about her involvement in the death of the victim. After 2 more hours of questioning, she was charged with 1st degree murder. In regard to a motive for the murder, there is a monetary and a revenge motive. The victim was known to have sexually molested both the defendant and her sister from an early age. He had also had them use drugs and alcohol at a young age and had been verbally abusive as well. An autopsy reveals the victim suffered injuries to the head from a baseball bat. The bat and other items were found with defendants and DNA testing connected them to the murder weapon. During the defendants holding period, she showed signs of depression and remorse.

2013

This defendant was having marital problems with her husband. The defendant calls a taxicab to pick her up. The taxicab also had another Fair rider which the victim would be the defendant a friend and the mutual friend asked if she want to go out and have drinks. The victim asks to talk to the defendant on the phone. The defendant asks who was speaking with. The defendant then asks if they could go to his residence to party, he stated yes. The Taxi arrived the defendant got in the back seat with the victim and he stated, "give me some sugar" and she did. The defendant advised the victim she was an alcoholic and she like to drink a lot. They arrived at the victims' residence, the defendant told the Taxi to pick her up in an hour and don't be late. They began drinking the defendant performed oral sex on the victim. The defendant went to the bathroom and left the door open and the victim came to the bathroom with his penis sticking outside his pants. The victim in the apartment became sexually aggressive towards her when the defendant came from the bathroom started kissing her on her face and neck. The defendant told the victim he was making her uncomfortable she did not want to have sex with him she just wanted to party. The victim went to the bathroom and returned with crack cocaine. He had hit the pipe once and then gave her a hit. Then the victim took the pipe back, because of this there was another fight. The victim wanted to have sex with her, requesting 5 minutes of her time. The defendant refused, and she pushed him away and he punched her in the mouth causing her tooth to come through her skin. She spit the blood from her mouth and punched him back. He said, "bitch you hit like a man." He began to assault her with his fist striking her in the face and head. There was no evidence of this. The victim forced her pants off at some point and brushed his penis against her face. The defendant fought back and looked for something to protect herself with. She saw an 8-inch screwdriver on the ground and stabbed him four times with it and stuck him up through the nose. The victim was yelling for help. The defendant felt disrespected He wrestled her to the ground and stabbed her twice with the screwdriver. She got the screwdriver back and blanked out. She learned she stabbed him 15 additional times. The defendant was convicted of 2nd degree murder 190 -237 months.

1991

Twin 27-year-old sisters have each been charged with three counts of first-degree murder in connection with the execution-style slayings of a woman and her two children, police said the twins both were arrested Friday night and charged with the slayings of three individuals the Police Chief said. The family's father was working at the time of the Wednesday killings, officials said. The bodies of mother and her two youngest children were found face down in their house, bound and shot with a rifle. The ex-husband and the twins are being held without bond, police said. First court appearance for the three is scheduled for Monday.

The State presented evidence tending to show the following. At the time the murders in this case were committed, defendant was involved in a relationship with defendant and had been so involved for five or six years. Throughout defendant's relationship with him he was married. They lived together in a mobile home during most of their marriage. For about a month prior to the homicides, however, she lived in a battered woman's shelter, although during other separations from him she lived with her parents. During the last separation, he lived with the twin, her two *844 children, and her twin sister, in a converted bus. During this period of separation, on 29 May 1990 at 11:30 p.m., she went to her parents' residence to return their car which she often borrowed. Her father drove her to work and then returned home to bed. The following morning, the father awoke at 3:45 a.m. in order to get ready for work. Shortly thereafter he left for work. When he returned to his home shortly after 1:00 p.m., he discovered that his daughter and two younger children, had been killed. They found the three bodies in the house. They had been tied up, gagged, and shot to death. They also found a broken windowpane in the carport door and a paper bag, to which cutout magazine letters which read "I told you about slapping my mother" were glued.

Defendant was tried capitally on indictments charging her with the first-degree murders, first-degree burglary; conspiracy to commit first-degree burglary and conspiracy to commit murder. The jury returned verdicts finding defendant guilty of all charges. Convictions for the three first-degree murders were based upon the theories of (1) premeditation and deliberation and (2) felony murder. At the capital sentencing proceeding for the first-degree murder convictions, the court submitted three aggravating and twenty-six mitigating circumstances. The sentencing findings were identical in each case and the jury recommended a sentence of death for each first-degree murder conviction. The trial court imposed the death sentences as recommended and imposed additional consecutive sentences of fifteen years, three years, and nine years for the additional convictions. For the

reasons discussed herein, we conclude that the guilt phase of defendant's trial was free from prejudicial error.

Once there was an inmate who just lost it, because the inmate they were in a relationship with was HIV and they didn't tell her. The inmate had been going down on her (oral sex) The inmate tried to end her life because of this. Inmate would stand at the fence calling out to the inmates in lock up saying, "I Love You." Then when they get out of lock up, most of the time they would end up in a fight, because they found out, they had been with another inmate, while they were in lock up, here we go, willie go around in circles.

This one inmate I think they were probably the oldest inmate at the time, her housing assignment was in the medical building. One day staff was talking with her and they told the staff "I'm going to fight you" the inmate was putting up her dukes, swinging at staff. LOL Responding to a code in Mental Health was terrible. Staff responding trying get on the elevator and others utilizing the stairwell, trying to get there by the quickest means possible. The elevator would place you right there, where you had to go and the stairwell, you would have to wait most of the time for someone to let you in the door, sometimes there would be staff waiting, there would be staff there waiting because they knew you were coming by stairs or elevator. All the administrative offices were located downstairs, so this one inmate decided she was going to flood her cell and the office underneath her was a hot mess. Inmates were smart though, they knew what to do, how to do and how long to do it to get the attention they wanted.

The staff in those office caught it during the day because, hose inmates beat and banged all day. There would be fights on the yard or in the dormitories; staff would respond we never knew what we would be against when we arrive at the location just be prepared. Sometimes other inmates would break up the fight. Inmates will fight with anything, irons, blow dryers whatever they could get their hands on to get the other inmate off them. There would be a lot of inmates standing around to see the show. Once staff arrives, they had to do crowd control and break up the fight. As I have said in the past there was never a boring minute, something was always going on.

1998

A Police officer went to investigate a suspicious vehicle that was parked in an apt. complex a few minutes later a female stated "excuse me" at that time the Officer was seated in the driver's seat of the police vehicle and looked up to observe a black female she stated "I just shot my husband" at which time she was stating that she shot her husband she was reaching under her shirt and pulling a gun from the front of her waistband. The suspect was attempting to give me the gun, at which time the officer immediately exited the vehicle and took control of the gun and the suspect. The Officer asked where she had shot her husband? The suspect she stated she had shot him in a car in the head. The officer later learned there was a witness in the car. He was in the back seat of the vehicle during the shooting. He stated the suspect was the victim's wife, he stated that the suspect had been stalking and harassing victim for a period of time. that he and the victim as well as, the victim's girlfriend had been together at his house with his girlfriend, and cousin. He got back in the back seat because he thought the victim would be picking up the cousin. As they sat in the car he never observed the suspect approach the car from any direction.

The next thing he heard were shots 4 or 5 and observed the victim, slumping backwards in the driver's seat. He stated that (positively identified) exited going west into the apartment complex.

2015

Two defendants were found guilty of second-degree murder. Both received the same sentence of a minimum of 20 years in prison and a maximum of 25 years. They said they plan to appeal.

Prosecutors claimed the male defendant, a 31-year veteran of the FBI, and his daughter,, had brutally murdered her 39-year-old husband. Experts testified that the physical evidence, in particular the blood spatter patterns, proved the victim suffered fatal blows to the head after he was already down.

The two defendants claimed the victim was choking her on the night of Aug. 2, 2015, when the male defendant intervened and hit him with a baseball bat. The male defendant testified that his daughter told him she also struck the victim with a paving stone that was on her nightstand, though father claims he didn't see it happen. They both said they were convinced the victim was trying to kill her and they were defending themselves and each other against him.

The medical examiner's report said the victim was hit at least 10 times and the cause of death was ruled blunt force trauma.

"To me, the choking did not occur," said the Jury foreman and another juror, agreed.

"Once you hit a certain point and you do not stop, manslaughter or self-defense goes off the table, "Once that point was matched where you could have stopped then and there, once the person was no longer an aggressor, if that were the case, and you continue, it's no longer self-defense."

Another major factor in their verdict decision, they said, was the gruesome crime scene photos. The first image of the victim's body she saw was so graphic that she vomited in the courtroom.

The three jurors said they believe she (daughter) and her father took some time after the victim died to conspire before they called 911, and they said the prosecution's argument that investigators said the two defendants didn't appear to have any injuries. She even believes the daughter struck her husband first with the paving stone while he was sleeping.

"I think at some point Dad came to help out and cover it up." "There was blood on the pillow and on the comforter. That may have been the first blow, and then it progressed from that point where he got out of bed and she might have struck him more than one time in bed."

"And when he got up and tried to protect himself, "I believe that's when the father had to intervene because of the size difference of his daughter and the victim."

The daughter did not take the stand at trial, but the jurors watched her closely throughout the trial and developed theories about her mental health.

1995

An inmate committed an assault on another inmate, by stabbing her in the left temple area penetrating two inches into the head. The assault was intended to kill and resulted in serious injury. On the date of the assault, the (victim) stated that inmate was lying on the bed talking with another inmate. The victim stated that the inmate was called on the intercom system. The inmate made the comment, "I'm tired of those mother fucker's watching me". Another inmate told the victim that the comment was directed towards her (victim). So, the victim replied back, then both inmates began arguing. According to the victim the inmate began choking her. The victim stated that the inmate had an ink pen in her hand which she got out her locker. The victim stated that the inmate stabbed her on the left side of her head with her right hand. The victim states that the inmate continued to choke her, throwing her on the floor, and proceeded to kick her. the victim was transported to the hospital.

We had an inmate that was being released from prison and somehow, they got the code to the intercom system. This inmate got on the intercom system and said "attention all dorms and post, attention all dorms and post" all staff and inmates "kiss my ass" something to that effect. We immediately knew who the inmate was an escorted them to lock up until they were released. The inmate was released from prison and returned back 1 or 2 years later with even more time. Upon them being returned they were placed back in lock up. That's why I continue to say all the time, to be mindful of everything going on around you always. Inmates are clever and sneaky; they watch everything you say and do. Inmates like for you to see their accomplishments especially graduating from GED, trade school, DART or Match Moms. I tried to go to most of their events to show my support and congratulate them on the job that they have done, this was a big deal to them. There was one inmate that was very talented with art and she drew several murals throughout the facility. Everywhere you turn, you would see this inmate craft, skill, painting of artwork it was phenomenal. I think they also did artwork at areas within the state buildings. This was their work assignment and they enjoyed it, they would come to me and let me know when they needed supplies and I would ensure they receive them. This inmate would also do their artwork for staff retirements, volunteer banquet, staff appreciation. There was one staff Social Worker that loved setting up for these events and she enjoyed it also. Everything always in sink and color coordinated, just a great decorator. We always had great food at these events, thanks to our kitchen supervisors working with the inmates to prepare the food. These things gave the inmates something to do. We also had the agriculture class that took care of the flowers and did flower arrangement for events. Things like this keep the inmate population busy. If they are busy doing something constructive, they don't have time to become involved in a whole lot of hoopla.

2002

Officers proceeded in making an arrest for a suspect with outstanding warrants. Officer was handcuffing the defendant as another Officer was arriving. The officer then proceeded to search the defendant for weapons. The defendant was then escorted to the police car and placed in the back seat, the car door was then closed. Officers had to obtain the warrants from headquarters and transport them to the magistrate's office. As the officer was in route to the headquarters, the other officer called out, an in-foot chase. The officer said the defendant was heading in the direction by the parking garage. The officer turned on Their sirens to go and assist. The officer then called that the defendant was headed back towards their vehicle. As officer was arriving at the scene they witnessed the defendant open the police car door and get in. The officer was going to block the other car, but mis judged her speed and ran up on the curb and hit a no parking sign. Unable to block the other car the officer got behind the defendant as they drove off. The defendant proceeded to run a red light at the intersection. Still heading North, the defendant then turned right reaching a speed of at least 70 mph. At the intersection all traffic had stopped due to seeing the chase. The defendant was traveling to fast to safely take the turn after the intersection. The car went slightly airborne and upon landing began to swerve into the oncoming lane. The vehicle hit the curb and started to tumble sideways. It appeared that the vehicle flipped at least two or three times. The officer stopped their vehicle next to the flipped car and ran to the left side of the car. The defendant was uninjured and fled the car running into the woods. The woods were so thick that it was hard to follow. A perimeter was set up pinning the defendant down. A k-9 unit arrived and tracked down the defendant inside of the perimeter. The defendant was arrested, and the medics assisted in treating them. The defendant charged and held on a $91,000 bond.

1996

In this joint trial, defendant was tried capitally for the first-degree murder, conspiracy to commit murder and solicitation to commit murder of the victim. The jury returned verdicts of guilty on all charges. After a capital sentencing proceeding, the jury failed to find the existence of the sole aggravating circumstance submitted and recommended a sentence of life imprisonment. The trial court sentenced this defendant accordingly and additionally imposed concurrent sentences of nine years' imprisonment each for the convictions of conspiracy to commit murder and solicitation to commit murder. The other Defendant was tried non-capitally, and the jury returned verdicts of guilty of first-degree *406 murder and guilty of conspiracy to commit murder of the victim. The trial court imposed the mandatory sentence of life imprisonment for the first-degree murder conviction and a concurrent sentence of nine years' imprisonment for the conviction of conspiracy to commit murder. We find no error and, therefore, uphold defendants' convictions and sentences.

The State's evidence at trial tends to show that defendant was married to the victim. The other defendant was defendant's daughter from a previous marriage. The actual shooter testified for the State pursuant to a plea arrangement. On the night of 24 December 1992, defendant's daughter told the defendant that her stepfather, the victim, physically abused her mother and her. Defendant's daughter then offered the defendant $15,000 in insurance proceeds and a truck if they would kill the victim. They agreed and drove to the defendant's trailer on Half-Mile Road. The defendant, armed with his .38-caliber pistol, got out of the car on the main road and waited for defendant to drive to the trailer, park the car and go inside. Defendant's daughter told defendant that she had found some people who would kill the victim, but defendant rejected the idea because she believed it would look strange if she was not hurt as well. The other two defendants then left.

Several weeks later, on 19 January 1993, defendants saw defendant walking down the road, and they pulled their car up beside him. Defendant got into the car, and defendant asked if he would still kill the victim for them. The defendant agreed on the condition that he would still receive the $15,000 and the truck in return; defendant said he would. While defendant's daughter drove the car to the trailer, defendant told the defendant that he would find the front door of the trailer unlocked and that when he entered the trailer, he would see the light from a television on in a bedroom and that in that bedroom, he would find the victim in the bed. Defendant also told the defendant he would find some money in the victim's pants pocket. Additionally, the defendant was instructed to take anything he wanted from the trailer and to break a window in order to make it look as if there had been a breaking and entering.

When defendants arrived at the main road in front of the trailer, the defendant got out and ran to the trailer. Defendants drove away. The defendant entered the trailer as he was told and shot the victim several times. After taking the victim's wallet, the defendant broke a window and then ran outside and across a field. Defendants arrived in the car, picked the defendant up and drove him away. After giving the defendant approximately $30 for a motel room, defendants pulled into a driveway and let the defendant out of the car.

YEAR 1997

About 10:00p.m., The female and three black males arrived at the home of the victim. The male victims and defendants were from up north and Canada except for the female who use to date one of the victims therefore she was known to them and she knew they were dealing drugs and from where. The female knocked on the door and they opened it to her, then her co-defendants pushed through the door with her. They were all armed with guns. There were five victims in the trailer, all young black males. Three men were made to lay face down on the living room floor and two men were forced at gun point into the bedroom while the gunmen searched for drugs and money. They weren't having much luck finding money, so they took the money out of the victims' wallets and a little powder residue was found outside the trailer, so they much have gotten some drugs, but the drugs weren't admitted to by the victims. It was reported that female's new boyfriend told one of the other defendants to kill one of the men on the floor to get them to talk. At that time the man placed a pillow over the victims' head and shot him. He was dead. The men in the bedroom heard this, jumped the gunmen and both jumped through the closed glass window and escaped. The remaining two victims in the living room both jumped up and attempted to escape. One went to the front door and was shot at 3 times but escaped with only a bullet hole through his pants zipper, the other went to the back door and was shot and killed.

The motive for this crime was monetary gain, according to the investigating officer. There was not an indication that the defendant and co-defendants were under the influence of drugs/alcohol at the time of the commission of the crime.

June 1999 the defendant pled guilty to 2 counts second degree murder, 2 counts armed robbery, second degree kidnapping and awdwwitk and received 2 active sentences of 150-189 months each, to be served at the expiration of each other. The female defendant was sentenced and given credit for 535 days prior to trial.

The male co-defendant pled guilty to 2 counts of first degree murder and received 2 life sentences to run at expiration of the other and awdw intent to kill and received 58-79 months active to run at the expiration of the last life sentence. Another male co-defendant pled guilty on September 1998 to 2 counts of second-degree murder and received 125-159 months for each case, to run at expiration of each other.

Other pertinent information included at this time is a third co-defendant, was also indicted for these crimes but has not been arrested at this time. It is believed that he is out of the country, possibly in Barbados. The defendant is serving a 99-year sentence in New York for murder.

YEAR 1998

May 1998 a 40-year-old white female was found murdered in her home. Upon an investigation by SBI and the sheriff department. When the husband of the victim had not been successful in reaching his wife by telephone. He contacted 911 to dispatch an officer to his residence to check on his wife. He was worried because he had talked with his daughter the night before who had stated that her mother was scared due to the fact that her son was mad and drugged up. She further stated that she and her son had an argument about him stealing checks out of her checkbook. According to the deputy's statement upon arriving at the residence he went around the house and looked through the window and observed what appeared to be a body lying on the floor in a pool of blood. He then went to the front door of the residence and forced it open. After entry was gained, the deputy observed the victim lying there with stab wounds to her body. The body was examined there were bruises around the neck and several stab wounds about the head. After a careful investigation it was determined that the son and his 14-year-old girlfriend had been operating the victim's) vehicle (mercury sable) special agents interviewed the people in the neighborhood. Several people had stated that the defendants had been hanging out together that evening before the murder. The deputy and county sheriff department received a tip as to where the son and girlfriend were. The girlfriend had called her mother. investigator had requested a warrant for the son and charged him with the murder of his mother after talking with both of the subjects it was indicated that they had planned to murder with a sword. In superior court on October 25, 2000, special agent testified that the victim had confronted her son about stealing checks from her checkbook. At that time, he became very angry with his mother and the argument escalated out of control. Both subjects went into the bedroom and began stabbing the victim several times with a sword in the neck, head and back. The female subject stabbed her repeatedly, according to the forensic pathologist report a blunt object was used to the head. Also, the cause of the death on the pathologist report was the loss of blood due to the stab wounds on the neck, chest and back and due to the blunt force injuries to the head. The murder weapon could not be located. The agents stressed to the court that the victim did not die immediately according to the autopsy report, it took her approximately six hours to die. It was stated in court that the victim was left alone in the last hours of her life, helpless to prevent her impending death.

Nov 24, 2010 my supervisor questioned me about an inmate, as to why they were moved down to another dorm. I told them at the time I could not remember. I knew it was about some confusion going on in the dorm. My supervisor stated, "well you know this inmate has written a grievance on you, about you moving them" and read the grievance to me. The inmate felt I was treating them unfairly and I had my favorites. I inform my supervisor; this was not so. My supervisor stated, "I have to have a reason for moving this inmate." I did I just couldn't remember what the reason was and I'm sure I had it in my notes somewhere. It was something going on with them and another inmate. Later I remembered, it was because of several inmates that were all involved in a relationship and causing confusion in the dormitory. I had warned this particular inmate and their girlfriend, that I would move them or lock them up, due to the confusion that they were creating in the dormitory. These inmates were moved, because they did not stand out like the other inmates, no other unit would house them. When you move inmates from unit to unit or dorm to dorm, you had to be careful, because you could mix oil and water, which is not a good combination and cause more problems. My supervisor is also constantly advising me to cut my tides with inmates that worked for me on special projects. I explained to her that there were not any ties or undue familiarity with this one inmate. This inmate was very vindictive. I told my supervisor the only reason I worked with her was because of the Warden/Deputy Warden, for the needs of the institution, so now you are going to label me, as being undue with this inmate. I told them I don't do undue, now if someone tell you I cursed out an inmate, it may have some validity to it. The Warden want a job done, to have showers in the units completed, tile replacement, grouting, filling in holes in the walls, that caused a terrible smell, due to mold and mildew. The more I'm asked to do and assist with, it was less appreciated, because of what other inmates say or complain about. They were just mad because they were not on the crew. I even talk to the Deputy Warden about this inmate getting in trouble, being in lock up and getting these write ups. I was trying my best to keep them out of trouble, at least until I could get these showers completed. This inmate was placed in lock up and received a write up for threaten staff. I went to segregation to talk to the inmate to find out what was going on. My supervisor got on me and stated, "why would you go to lock up to see that inmate?" Well Why not? They worked with me in doing a project for the needs of the institution. THE NEEDS OF THE INSTITUTION! was the a constantly use phase. Then I was asked do I go up there to see all the inmates that get locked up, Yeah, when I make rounds, but they don't work on this project with me for the Warden either. Then I was told not to talk to this inmate. My supervisor says to me, "well there seems like there may be a little bit of undue going on here." I jumped up from the chair and stated, "the SHIT you say." I just left out the office, I was done. This inmate was then released from lock up after 1800 and was placed in another unit. I was informed the next day. I conducted some inmate moves, to get this inmate moved back to her previous unit, where she was originally housed. The other units will not accept housing for certain inmates. So here we go again Why I move the inmate back. I told them the unit manager was already having a fit. I move inmate back. My supervisor says, "well you should have left them were they were." As I was trying to explain to them, she already knows the other units will not take certain inmates and this inmate is one of those. My supervisor states "well I'm moving her back." I told them fine, I don't care where you move her to, I don't have a problem managing my inmates.

NOVEMBER 2004

Police responded to a residence that was being broken into. When the police arrive, they pushed the door open and they could see a black male lying on the floor, with blood surrounding the victim. The defendant was friends with one of the victims and had brought two other defendants with her from another state, to rob the victims. Both defendants were armed with guns when the entered the victim's residence. The defendant (female) was in the back bedroom with the victim. Two of the victims were shot in the living room. The victim in the bedroom was able to barricade himself behind the door. The victim fired through the door with a 9 MM. The defendant escaped through the window in the bedroom and ran to her car, where she waited for the other two subjects. They then returned to the previous state. The defendant was arrested and returned to the state. The defendant receives a sentence of 313-396 months 1st degree murder and 1st degree burglary.

Working Shift most of the inmates were out of the building, at work projects. Then there were inmates medically unassigned, inmates unassigned waiting to be assigned to a project assignment, to being on bed rest. Inmates on bed rest meant just that. You were going to be in the building, you don't get all those privileges of being out on the grounds, going to the canteen and activities. Some inmates would get bed rest because they didn't want to go to work, hang out with their friend etc. Staff had to be on their toes 24 hrs a day 7 day a week. They would injure themselves like close their hands in the locker. There were a lot of locker incidents. The dining room there was so many accidents with the workers in that area, Inmates and them food carts rolling on their feet or getting their hand smashed it was always something, there should have just been medical provided for them only.

NEWSPAPER CLIP 2002

Defendant was charged in indictments with the first-degree murder of the victim, and possession of a firearm by a convicted felon. The jury returned guilty verdicts on both charges, with special verdicts finding first-degree murder by premeditation and deliberation and by lying in wait. Following a capital sentencing hearing, the jury returned a verdict recommending life in prison without parole. The court sentenced defendant accordingly and imposed a concurrent sentence of twenty-one to twenty-six months for the firearm charge.

Defendant appeals.

At trial, defendant conceded that she had been in a troubled relationship with the victim and that she had been present when he was shot to death. Defendant admitted that she had brought the firearm to the scene, was holding it when it fired, and must have pulled the trigger. The medical examiner testified that the victim suffered two bullet wounds, one of which entered his chin from an indeterminate distance. The other bullet had entered the front of his chest from only a few inches away, and the exit wound indicated that, at the time he was shot, Brown's back was pressed up against something firm, like the floor. The victim had also suffered a head laceration, which could have been caused by a fall down the stairs or by a blow from the butt of a gun. The victim's jacket had been pulled up behind his back and his pockets had been turned inside out and emptied.

The cords to Brown's phone and caller ID box in the bedroom were cut.

NEWSPAPER CLIP 2004

A Raleigh woman will spend the rest of her life in prison in connection with a deadly shooting last summer. Defendant was convicted Thursday of first-degree murder and sentenced to life in prison. The victim was found fatally shot in an SUV that was parked near a townhouse off Leesville Road.

Newspaper clip 1992

Victim insurance agent was reported missing in 1992 by his wife. The local Crime Stoppers organization asked for the public's help with the killing. In response a caller offered two names. Investigation uncovered an elaborate conspiracy. For about a year, the defendant had been trying to get another defendant to kill her husband. She said the defendant beat her, among other things. The defendant eventually agreed to do the deed and enlisted yet another accomplice, bringing them into the plan. The hit-team, two defendants set up a meeting, with assistance of the victim's wife, with their victim pretending to be interested in an insurance policy. Prior to the meeting, the victim stopped by a local hotel where his wife was attending a cosmetics convention. His body was later found on a road, he had been shot in the stomach with a shotgun. The wife and her two agents three were arrested in connection to victim's murder.

One of the two defendants were sentenced to death for actually pulling the trigger and was eventually executed in 2002. The other defendant was sentenced to 30 years. Pleading to avoid the death penalty, the victim's wife received life in prison.

As a result of victim's murder, a 1973 death in the family, of a four-year-old boy that had been ruled accidental was re-examined in a new light. The defendant had delivered her stepson, asphyxiated from dry cleaning plastic that, according to stepmom he had swallowed. Plastic was removed from the child's throat, but he did not survive. Two decades after the "accident" the boy's body was exhumed. The autopsy ruled the death a homicide. The defendant was charged with his murder, was convicted and sentenced once again to life in prison.

Author of a book on the defendant's criminal career, *"Fatal Kiss,"* (2005), believes she has a total of three murders to her credit. Her first victim was husband #1, He was shot to death in 1967 and the case was ruled a suicide. Yet, as the author points out, some evidence in the case never added up. "He was right-handed, but the gun was in his left hand," notes the author, summing up her subject's career, observing: "She got away with that," she added. "She killed three people."

November 29, 2010 my supervisor had inmate in her office and was asking me about a request the inmate had put in, to move back to the unit, because she had been down the hill in another dorm for 4 months. I informed them that my sgts handle all the movements request; they actually get with me prior to moving anyone. I informed them later that the inmate came to her to get moved back to the unit, because that's what another inmate told her, to go to you because that's how she got moved back to the unit. Inmates playing both ends against the middle.

Officers are posted in buildings classified as 208 building but the normal was 300. Most of the time the Officers were there by themselves, due to a shortage of staff, they would do their jobs to the best of their ability, considering. There were 3 of these buildings with 4 quads on each end of the building. The quad bulletin boards had to remain updated at all times with Disciplinary, Legal Aid, grievance policies, medical was also added. You could put this information up and go back the next day, it would be gone or the inmates would remove it, write on it or tear it. These areas also included an administration area between the two dormitories that included a unit/assist manager, Sergeant, case worker, social worker, medical (PRNs). a conference room, laundry room with assigned laundry room attendants for each dorm, canteen where inmates allowed to purchase food items and supplies, storage area with cleaning supplies stored in locked cabinets. Each building had a yard area in the back, with picnic tables for the inmates to sit at. Most of the time there was not a yard officer, because there was always a shortage of staff. Inmates knew this, so they would gamble, have sex, do drugs, fight, assault other inmates. Inmates would pass you or walk up to you with bruises or scratches. When you ask them, what happen? their response would be they done it to themselves. This was to keep their girlfriend, friend or associate from getting into trouble and going to lock up. When the Officers see this, they would report it to their Sgt or Management, who then would investigate to see what happen, this would usually result in someone being placed in lock up. There was always staff assigned to the yard by the lineup, but once the Capt /Lt had to fill in all the holes from staff call out, it would leave the yard with no Officer. At this point the Sgt or Unit Manager / Asst would have to go out and assist on the grounds, between all the other duties they had to complete. In one of the dormitories there were special work assignments like MATCH **M**others **A**nd **T**heir **Ch**ildren. There were strict guidelines in order to be in in this program. You really had no chances at all. First time you screwed up that was it, no more MATCH. The program gave some hope to the mothers of children knowing they would be able to see and bond with their child, even though they were in prison. This made the inmate work harder to stay out of trouble, be infraction free and try to do the right thing. Then you had the DART program **D**rugs **A**lcohol **R**esearch **T**reatment inmates were assigned to the program as court ordered, because they had some type of interactions with drugs, alcohol or both. Now it is referred to as ACDP **A**lcohol **C**hemical **D**ependency **P**rogram. It is there to help assist that individual if they have alcohol or drug issues. A lot of inmates would come in and say they were court ordered to complete the program 90 days and they would be released. There were still others that did the program and continued to seek out drug while in the system. Inmates would still find a way to do drugs, alcohol, buying, stealing medications, syringes, to support their habits. Inmates would self-mutilate themselves, use their own feces to rub in an open wound, to cause infection, to get pain medication. Inmates would be drug tested on a regular basis or tested from a computer-generated list or if they were under suspicion. The staff was trained to conduct this testing of collecting urine samples from the inmates. Staff would collect urine from inmates early in the morning, when they were just waking up. Once this happen the drug testing procedures has begun. The inmates on the list would have to stay under strict observation, until they provide a urine sample. The only fluids they were allowed to have, was so many ounces of water. Inmates would always figure out a way around this to throw staff off, if they were not paying attention. Inmates would buy urine from other inmates, put it in a medicine bottle insert it in their vaginal area. When they went to the restroom to provide their urine, with the Officer standing right there, the inmate would remove the top from the bottle and release the urine in the cup provided. Inmates would go in the bathroom and have a bowel movement, thinking the Officer would leave, but that was not going to happen. Inmates nearly poisoning themselves, going as far to drinking Clorox or cleaning chemicals, because they knew they were dirty and their test would come back inconclusive. Inmates knew if their test came back positive, it was an automatic ticket to jail (lockup). Some inmates just could not produce urine because of some medical term they use. If they could not produce urine in a certain amount of time, they went to lock up. Inmates would refuse to go in the ADCP program, they were informed they did not have a choice because it was court ordered and if they refused they will go to lock up. There was only one quad when this program began, but another quad was added because there were so many inmates being assigned. The other quad remaining was housing regular work assignment. Inmates obtained contraband items mostly from the outside, through visitation or dirty staff, putting everyone staff and inmates at risk or in danger with some of the effects, it would take on inmates. The dirty staff would stand right there beside you, grin and laugh in your face and you had no idea. The best cure for that GERM was to turn them in, trust no one in this setting. Always remember CYA **C**over **Y**our **A**ss. That was one of the vital lessons I learned when I first started working at Women's Prison. If you observe your coworkers engaging in undue familiarity or anything that just didn't seem right it was your **D**uty **t**o **R**eport. If you didn't report it you were just as guilty as the person committing the act, because you knew about it and chose not to report it.

YEAR OF 1997

This offender was (DWLR) driving while license revoked, she states she never had a driver license, she drives with no license and was stopped by an officer on 2 occasions. The offender committed an assault with a deadly weapon, when her and this lady got into an argument over some drugs. She states she assaulted her with an alcohol bottle and knocked out one tooth. The assault on a government official was the result of the officer taking a stem pipe from her while being in a drug area. She states she spit on the officers and kick them in their testicles. Drug paraphernalia charge was because she was in a drug infested area and the officer saw her with the stem pipe. The DWI charge was the officer stopped her because she was swerving, she was putting out a cigarette in the ashtray. The offender refuses the breathalyzer test. Resisting an officer, she would not cooperate with the officer after getting into an argument with a lady over drugs. The possess and consume beer/wine was a result of the officer stopping her as she walked down the street drinking beer. The offender stated she had been out smoking crack cocaine and was trying to get home before her husband did and ended up hitting a car in the rear. Left the scene of the accident on foot and was later arrested in the neighborhood.

YEAR OF 1989

This offender committed common law robbery, larceny of auto, driving while impaired, failure to stop for an accident, property damage, assault on a Law Enforcement Officer, injury to personal property.

The offender did steal and take and carry away $300 in cash from the person and presence of the victim by means of an assault consisting of forcible and violent taking of property. The officer received a call and upon arrival at the address they spoke to the victim, who appeared to have been drinking a lot. The victim stated a black female he knew and a black male he thinks he knew, beat him down and took his money. The victim stated that the female held him while the male hit him with his fists and took $300 in cash. He then staggered back to his residence. The defendant was charge where she pled guilty to common law robbery, several other non-related charges including larceny of auto, driving while impaired, failure to stop for an accident, assault on LEO and injury to personal property. The offender was sentenced to active term of 10 years.

In 1993 this offender approached a victim who was out walking and said today was her birthday and wanted to know if the victim was going to wish her a happy birthday and tried to hug the victim. The male subject walking with her stuck something sharp into the victim's shoulder. They both told the victim "give up everything they had". The victim knew the female from working at the Arts Council where she had done community service about a year ago. The victim was shown a photographic line up consisting of six polaroid photographs of black females. The victim immediately identified the suspect, who the victim had known for some time. A warrant was issued for the defendant charging them with robbery with a dangerous weapon. The defendant was arrested on probation. The defendant was sentenced to 10 years active with 227 days spent in custody.

YEAR 2002

RALEIGH, N.C. -- Defendant facing a possible death sentence for the killing of his victim in 2002, hanged himself in his Prison cell.

Staff found inmate's body about 2 p.m., said North Carolina Department of Correction spokesman. One of defendant's attorneys, said he hanged himself. he left no note.

Medical workers tried to resuscitate the 35-year-old, at the prison hospital, but he was declared dead at 2:37 p.m. The spokesperson refused to give details about the suicide, citing a State Bureau of Investigation probe into the death.

Police arrested the defendant a North Carolina Department of Agriculture fertilizer technician, Oct. 19 after a DNA sample they obtained from his office matched semen found at the crime scene.

Investigators found victim's body May 21, 2002, in a room of her Lake Lynn apartment. Police said they think the defendant entered the victim's apartment by removing a screen and climbing through a window as she slept. Once inside, police said, he bound her and sexually assaulted her. Police said he later choked her with a wire or rope.

Wake District Attorney said the defendant's death meant the victim's family would be spared a lengthy and intense murder trial. The defendant's death ended a murder case that gripped Raleigh for years.

Born in New Jersey, he moved to Michigan with his mother after his parents divorced. Neighbors, relatives and former teachers described him as painfully shy.

He graduated from Michigan State University in East Lansing with a zoology degree in 1995 and moved to Raleigh in 2000 to work for the Agriculture Department.

The victim lived in an apartment complex separated from the defendant by a few hundred feet of woods.

A woman with large brown eyes and a bright smile, she was a native of Rocky Mount, Va. She moved with her family and a friend to Raleigh in 2001 after her graduation from College. The trio rented a first-floor apartment in the Bridgeport complex off Lynn Road and the victim worked for an IBM contractor.

Detectives said they believe that the defendant was a peeping Tom who was seen peering into the victim's window a few weeks before her killing.

When police searched the defendant home, they found an extensive pornography collection, at least 12 firearms, handcuffs and dozens of knives.

Investigators found several of the victim's personal effects in the defendant's apartment -- including a laundry basket, bank statements and documents about her student loans, Assistant District Attorney said. Also, inside the apartment were clipped newspaper articles about the victim's death.

Recent ballistics tests on one of the guns conclusively linked him to the October 1999 killing of another victim in the driveway of her Lansing, Mich., home. The shell casing and bullet recovered from the Michigan crime scene matched the gun perfectly. Police seized directions to other women's homes, and documents containing the names of a score of women.

Inmates would do whatever they could to get high. They would make (HOOCH) with yeast and fruit. They would get these items from the dining hall, by way of the dining hall workers most of the time or just save the fruit they received with their meals. They would put it in any container that would hold it, cover it up place it in a common area, so no one would get charge with an offense. When it started fermenting it smelled so loud. The entire area would be search or a search would be conducted, most of the time it was in the dayroom, bookshelves, trash can, bathroom. I was so afraid one day they would consume this stuff and we would have horror on our hands, with these inmates getting poison from this stuff. There was some confiscated once and placed in an office, it exploded, and it smelled like a winery for a long time.

Inmates would go to visitation to visit their families, there were only 3 approved adult visitors for each visit. When the families came to visit, they seem to have brought their children and all the neighborhood children with them. Unfortunately, there was not a limit on how many children could visit under the age 18. It would be more children at visitation than adults. Children running around doing what kids do, not listening. Some inmates would use their kids as a mule to get contraband in. The adults would come in and kiss for at least 10 seconds, which was too long, but long enough for them to pass that contraband mouth to mouth. Visitors would go to the restroom and hide contraband. If the right staff was not in there to search after visitation, inmates would pick up the contraband and not deliver it as plan and either use it or sell it for their own gain. Then there would really be a disruption on the grounds or in the dormitory. The visitors would come in loaded; you could smell the alcohol before they got to you. What made it so bad, they would want to argue the fact, well I drank last night. It didn't matter if you consumed alcohol last week, if my staff or I could smell it you would not be entering the prison not on my tour. Suboxen and cigarettes were the big sellers on the compound. Suboxen could come in pills or strips. If they weren't buying medication on the compound from the inmates, that would get their meds in a 30-day supply, especially pain meds. This was never a good idea, but because the population had gotten so large this was the plan, self-medication. There were some inmates would have to receive their meds in a liquid form, that was dispensed to them. When they took this medication, they would hold it some kind of way in their throat, and then spit it out in a bottle to sell to another inmate, which is really gross. There was a trailer that the inmates in DART program was assigned to for class, but it soon got ran down and the program grew with all these inmates assigned and was eventually relocated to another building called the programs building. This building had case managers, Chaplains, Cosmetology, main canteen and DART (ACDP). There were also classes for ADCP held in Diagnostic area later. The inmates that completed the class would be removed from the DART quad, place in a regular quad and assigned to a work project. The Sgt in the unit would bring a list to master control, where all internal and external moves would occur on the weekend, inmates completed would be move out and inmates beginning would be placed back in.

1985

The evidence introduced during a jury trial tended to show that on the afternoon of 26 October 1983, defendant took her ten-month-old son, to the emergency room, she placed the baby in a nurse's arms and said, "I think my baby died yesterday, but I think he took a breath today." It was determined that the baby had been dead for some time. The baby's body was stiff and was bruised in various places.

At the hospital, defendant told medical personnel "that she had occasionally slapped the child and had slapped the baby around because the baby made her nervous; that they were very poor, that they hadn't had a lot of food to eat and that the baby was fussing and crying and that she had never hit the child with her fist and ... that the bruises that were on the child then were not places that she had hit the child but places where the blood had been pooled after it died." Certain witnesses for the State testified that defendant showed very little emotion, seemed very nervous, but not remorseful, after the incident.

1992

Defendant 37 was convicted in December 1990 for plotting the March 17, 1990 choking murder of her 48-year-old husband. The defendant's boyfriend, and another participant, were convicted of killing the victim by strangling him with a necktie, a baby blanket and rope. The defendant was convicted of first-degree murder in May 1991 and sentenced to life in prison. The other defendant pleaded guilty to second-degree murder shortly after the other defendant's trial and received a life sentence in exchange for testifying against the defendant and the boyfriend. According to testimony at trial, the defendant called the other two defendants to come over when her husband fell asleep. She waited in the other room while her husband was killed. A woman convicted of plotting the murder of her husband will get a new sentencing hearing, the state Supreme Court ruled Thursday.

The defendant's first-degree murder conviction stands, but the court said the Alamance County jury that recommended the death penalty should have been told that she had no history of previous crimes. When a jury weighs the death penalty against life in prison, it must consider factors that help make the choice clearer. Whether the defendant had a previous criminal history is one of those factors.

The District Attorney said he was disappointed that the defendant's sentence didn't stand, but he was glad the conviction was upheld. He said he will read the court's ruling to study the sentencing problem.

NEWS PAPER CLIP 2000

At trial, the evidence tended to show that the couple married in 1991 and subsequently lived in several different states as the Captain was stationed at Air Force bases around the country. In 1999, the couple moved to, where the Captain was posted at the Air Force Base and Defendant was employed by a psychologist, as she worked toward getting her own permanent license as a psychologist. Throughout this time, the Captain was often deployed overseas and away from home for long stretches of time, and the marriage struggled.

In early 2000, Defendant met United States Army Sergeant a Special Forces soldier, via the Internet and began an extramarital affair with him. In June 2000, Defendant rented her own apartment and lived separately from the Captain: the two started marital counseling in July while also going through a trial separation. In October, Defendant reconciled with the Captain, moving back into their home and telling her employer, that she planned to end her affair with the Sergeant. In November, the Sergeant sent e-mails to Defendant indicating he was unhappy about the possibility of their relationship ending and Defendant's remaining with her husband. On 9 December 2000, Defendant met and engaged in sexual relations with the Sergeant, after telling the Captain she was going there to celebrate her birthday with a graduate school classmate. On 17 December 2000, Defendant and the Captain traveled from Fayetteville to Cary with her employer, his wife, and another couple, for a dinner to celebrate the holidays. Around 9:00 or 9:30 p.m., as the group prepared to leave the restaurant, Defendant went to the restroom and made a cell phone call to the Sergeant, who was watching a video with his estranged wife and mother-in-law. After the phone call, the Sergeant put on cold-weather clothing and left the house.

Meanwhile, Defendant and the Captain took the other couple back to her employer's office, where they had left their car, arriving around 10:30 p.m. Thereafter, Defendant and her husband left the parking lot but returned approximately ten to fifteen minutes later after Defendant "remembered that she needed a reference book from her office to prepare for two book reports due the next day." Defendant later told the police that the Captain waited outside while she went inside the office to get the books. Shortly thereafter, she heard gunshots, ran outside, and found the Captain, unresponsive, at the bottom of the steps outside of the building. Defendant stated that because she had accidentally locked her keys inside the building when she went outside, she ran to a late-night video store about a block away to get help. The Captain died as a result of five gunshot wounds, including one fired at close range just behind his left ear.

Following the Captain's death, the Defendant continued her relationship with Sergeant, including taking a trip together. Police later linked the Sergeant to a semiautomatic pistol that was of the same model used to kill the Captain. However, after the Sergeant learned that the police wanted to obtain the pistol for ballistics testing, he reported that his vehicle had been broken into on base and the weapon stolen.

As a result of his statements regarding the pistol, military authorities charged the Sergeant with making a false official statement, false swearing, and obstruction of justice. Around 20 February 2001, he was placed into pre-trial confinement at a military facility. The Sergeant was later charged with and convicted by a General Court-Martial of murder and conspiracy to commit murder in the death of the Captain and sentenced to life in prison without parole.

On 21 May 2002, Defendant was indicted for first-degree murder and conspiracy to commit first-degree murder in the death of the Captain. However, around the date of the indictment, Defendant, who had moved since the murder, left from there, reportedly to "start a new life." She moved where she rented an apartment and had plastic surgery performed under an assumed name. Files and documents found in her apartment indicated Defendant had a long-range plan to create several false identities and essentially to "disappear."

Police located and arrested Defendant in August 2002, and her trial began on 27 September 2004. At the conclusion of the nearly three-month trial, the jury returned verdicts of guilty of first-degree murder by aiding and abetting, and of conspiracy to commit first-degree murder. The trial court sentenced Defendant to life in prison without parole. Book: The Real Gone Girl: The true story

2000

A jury decided that this defendant must die for hiring a hit man to kill her husband in 1999, ignoring pleas that domestic abuse forced the murder.

defendant, a mother of two, cried as the verdict was read Thursday. Under state law, her lawyers immediately filed an appeal. `I don't know if justice has been served but there's been a little vindication, a little satisfaction,' said the sister of the victim. ``She can't do this to anyone else.'

There was minimal sympathy for her former sister-in-law, who said defendant ``put on' a stoic, emotionless appearance so the jurors would think she was a victim with mental illnesses.

Prosecutors argued that the defendant's motive was greed: She hoped to collect more than $100,000 from her husband's life insurance policy. The defendant spent more than six months looking for a hit man before paying someone $150. The victim was killed March 24, 1999. His chest, arms and back were torn up by at least six bullets. He died on the living room floor of his home. The defendant, though, insisted to investigators and the jury that her husband constantly abused her both verbally and physically, creating a marriage so unbearable and inescapable that she had no choice but to have him killed. Hoping to avoid the death sentence in favor of life in prison without parole, defense attorneys asked leniency for their client because she willingly gave a confession, then led investigators to the gunman's home. They also stressed her bouts with serious depression and a personality disorder stemming from sexual abuse and parental neglect as a child. Defense attorney did not deny his client's role in the murder during closing arguments. At the time of the murder, the defendant ``suffered from and was influenced by several mental disorders' stemming from her lifetime of abuse, ``None of which are reasons (to kill) but are taken into consideration.'

The defendant becomes the sixth woman, awaiting death by lethal injection. After several hours of police interrogation, both defendants confessed. They were both convicted of first-degree murder. In January 2001 Defendant received a death sentence in October 2000 but it was commuted to life without parole.

Master Control this pretty much was the brain of the institution. You had to be mentally capable of running this area. It took a special group of people to run this area. There was always so much going on at one time, doing movements, answering phones, issuing out keys. The Officer would have to basically play musical chairs, to get movements done, when there was no bed space, and this occurred often. You could not just have just anyone in this area, it was critical. There was a staff that had been trained in this area; we thought was going to be good at this assignment, this did not work out to well. They would sit there all day doing everything besides movements. When it was time for count it was screwed up from high heaven. They had to be removed this could not happen. This area had Capt. Lt. Sgt. Assist Supt. along with mailroom, records, academic school, MATCH, visitation, grievances and disciplinary hearing held once or twice a week, your count, movements internal and external, admissions, discharges the only time things may slow down was on the weekend it then. This person was special, you had to have knowledge of the screens, what to look at and how to utilize them. If the count or movement was not balancing out you have to be able to figure out where the problem was within a reasonable time, if not you were not relieved. There was some staff that made the count work, instead of knowing it was right, all the time putting their JOB on the line. There were several staff that was trained in this area, but it proved to be a little much for a few. When at the end of the day, the count would be tore to hell and back, you would have to get someone to come up there to straighten the mess out. Be able to communicate with other staff outside the confines of women's prison, to get the job done. This person stays busy from the time they come on at 6:00 until they leave at 6:00 or pass the hour. In the control center we also had a refrigerator, back by the holding cell for staff use. Staff would store their food and drinks. Then staff began complaining that someone was eating their food or taken their food. So, I'm like someone must be really hungry to take someone else's food. However, there was an exit door right by the refrigerator, that leads out to the bicentennial yard area, where most of the inmates set. Later on we found out the inmates would come in and take the food items out of the refrigerator, by accessing this door which was off limits to the inmates entrance, unless they were escorted by staff and go out on the bicentennial yard and share the items with their friends or peers and staff was blaming each other. The inmates would also take items out, while they were sitting there waiting to be seen by the DHO Disciplinary Hearing Officer. It was always explained to me that an ink pen can cause a lot of damage. This was a very true statement. If staff wrote up an inmate, it could jeopardize several things, where the inmate was concerned, classification, good time, gain time. Sometimes staff would write up inmates and the inmate would be released the next day. If the write up was processed, the inmate's release date would be pushed up, anywhere up to 30 days. Some inmates live and thrive on getting written up daily. Inmates commit infractions and receive disciplinary, if they pled not guilty, they would be seen by the DHO, who would review the allege infraction giving the inmate and opportunity to explain what happen, then they are given their punishment or found not guilty. These ladies did not like to come to control for disciplinary. I would get on the intercom system and call out their names, advise them they had 2 minutes to get to control. If they did not show, I would go looking for them on the yard. Once I located them, I would restrain them and escort them to the area. Once I did this a couple of times, I did not have a problem with these inmates reporting to disciplinary hearing. They didn't like being embarrassed on the compound in front of their friends. We would always learn that before going through the disciplinary process, that the inmate would receive verbal counseling on several occasions and sometimes for the same infraction, before actually receiving disciplinary. This was our tool for correction measures, however sometimes it just didn't work for some inmates. Inmates would get write ups that would be two pages long in the system. They just didn't care. The charge for each write up was $10.00. Once they receive so many write ups, they could be referred to be placed on intensive control, if we had space to place them on long term segregation. Inmates would be place on this control from 60 to 90 days, some it would deter and some it would not. When they did get out, they would be happy to be free again to see their little friends. We also tried to utilize voluntary work when an offender committed a rule violation, which they would prefer rather than a write up. This was how I tried to correct bad behavior as well as some other staff. The inmate had to volunteer; at this rate you could get areas of the institution cleaned. You could kill two birds with one stone, keeping inmates busy and getting some much-needed work done. Then there came a time, where there was nowhere to lock up inmates because lock up was full. There were several inmates with segregation time that would expire, because there was nowhere to house them in segregation, because of the capacity. The disciplinary seg days overrode our lock up space, then we began to play musical chairs, let this one out and lock this one up. It had gotten so bad, that the inmates would get in a fight, they knew we would let out someone to make room and this was how they would get their friends out of segregation, until we caught on to it. We would try and lock up the aggressor or just not lock up neither one and place them in separate buildings, which was not sending a good message to the other population inmates. Then this gave the inmates the idea that they could get in trouble or fight and not got to lock up, due to space. Inmates knew there was not lock up space, so what they would do if one of their friends was in segregation or someone they wanted out of lock up. They would stage fights that we would release inmates to lock inmates up. The inmates were playing their own game of musical chairs, most of the time they knew what we would do before we done it. LOL!!

1999

Defendant was indicted on 4 January 1999 for two counts each of first-degree murder, first-degree kidnapping, and robbery with a dangerous weapon, as well as one count each of conspiracy to commit first-degree murder, conspiracy to commit first-degree kidnapping, and conspiracy to commit robbery with a dangerous weapon. In a second multicount indictment issued 25 January 1999, defendant was also indicted for attempted first-degree murder, conspiracy to commit first-degree murder, assault with a deadly weapon with intent to kill inflicting serious injury, first-degree kidnapping, and robbery with a dangerous weapon. Defendant was tried capitally, and the jury found her guilty of all charges, specifically finding her guilty of both murders on the basis of premeditation and deliberation and under the felony murder rule. Following a capital sentencing proceeding, the jury recommended a sentence of death for each of the murders, and the trial court entered judgments accordingly. The trial court also sentenced defendant to consecutive terms of imprisonment for each of the nine other felony convictions.

The State's evidence at trial tended to show that defendant was one of nine gang members who set out to steal a car on the evening of 16 August 1998. The gang members gathered at and then left from defendant's residence.

The gang needed money, and the members decided they would steal a car, drive it into the window of a pawn shop, and steal the property in the pawn shop. Several gang members, including defendant, went to the local Wal-Mart to steal some toiletry items and clothing, and to buy bullets for the occasion. The bullets were taken to the home where the tips were painted blue, the color identified with a gang, with fingernail polish from defendant's bedroom.

Soon thereafter, defendant and an unidentified deaf black male who was not part of the gang drove to a neighborhood location and dropped them off with instructions to find a victim to rob, to steal the victim's car, to put the victim in the trunk of the car, and then to return to defendant's trailer within an hour and a half. Defendant provided them with a gun, and then she and the deaf black male drove away, leaving the other defendants.

The three gang members walked around looking for someone to rob, and at about 12:30 a.m. on Monday, 17 August, they spotted their victim leaving the Bojangles where she was the manager. The defendants abducted the victim at gunpoint and drove around in her car with her in the backseat for a period of time before they stopped the car and put her in the trunk, also robbing her of her jewelry and money. They returned to defendant's trailer, where the remainder of the gang gathered around the car while discussing what to do with victim.

Thereafter, with victim still in the trunk, the defendants, got into the victim's car and drove her to the Lake, a location on the military base. Defendant told victim to get down on one knee. Defendant attempted to fire the gun at the victim, but it jammed. Defendant said, "hold up" and tried to unjam the gun. Defendant then raised the gun again, this time to the level of the victim's waist, and fired the bullet into the victim's right side. After the shot knocked the victim down onto her stomach, defendant shot her seven more times. The final shot went through the victim's glasses, grazed her eyelid, and hit her thumb. The victim pretended to be dead. She was discovered the next morning by a passerby and was subsequently taken to a hospital.

The victim testified that no one told defendant to shoot her, the gun jammed before any shots were fired, it was defendant who told her to go down on one knee, there was no break in the firing of the bullets sufficient for defendant to have handed the gun to any other person to shoot her, and it was defendant who shot her.

After defendant shot the victim and left her for dead, the gang members returned to defendant's trailer, where they concluded that they needed a second car. The defendants rode around in victim's car, ultimately targeting a car driven by another victim and her passenger. The gang trapped the victim's car at the end of a dead-end road, and defendant handed a gun to another defendant, telling him to "go do what you got to do." Defendants, then drove away in the first victim's car after defendant directed other three defendants to be back at her trailer in forty-five minutes.

The defendants forced the two victims into the trunk at gunpoint, and then the three returned to defendant's trailer with the women in the trunk. At one point during the drive, the car was stopped so that the gang members could open the trunk and rob the women of their jewelry.

Upon the return to defendant's trailer, the entire gang surrounded the car and discussed who would kill the women. Despite the women's pleas for mercy, the entire gang, half in one car and half in other car, drove to a location where the women were forced out of the trunk and executed, each by a blue-tipped bullet to the brain. Queen shot one of the women, and defendant shot the other. The gang members once again returned to defendant's trailer.

After talking for a while, the group split up, with instructions to return by 3:30 p.m. Sometime around dawn, Defendant received news that some bodies had been found. Seven members of the gang, including defendant, subsequently fled to the Beach using victim's cell phone to place calls to defendant's trailer. Two of the defendants did not accompany the gang to the Beach.

On Tuesday, 18 August, two defendants were apprehended in the first victim's car by police officers. On Wednesday, 19

August, defendant, the other defendants were apprehended and arrested at the motel, in a room rented by defendant. One of the women was able to survive and would testify against the defendant who would be sentenced to death.

1995

Defendant was indicted 30 January 1995 for first-degree murder and felonious child abuse. In September 1996, defendant was tried capitally and found guilty of first-degree murder on the basis of malice, premeditation and deliberation; on the basis of torture; and under the felony murder rule, she was also found guilty of felonious child abuse. Following a capital sentencing proceeding, the jury recommended a sentence of death for the first-degree murder conviction, and the trial court entered judgment accordingly. The trial court also sentenced defendant to three years' imprisonment for felonious child abuse.

After consideration of the assignments of error brought forward on appeal by defendant and a thorough review of the transcript of the proceedings, the record on appeal, the briefs, and oral arguments, we find no error meriting reversal of defendant's convictions or sentences.

The State's evidence tended to show that the victim had numerous injuries extending all over her body, including bruises on her face, cheeks and jaw, chin, forehead, sides of her neck, collarbones, over the front of her chest, on her back, over her right flank, her buttocks, upper and lower legs, her eyelid, and on her shins. Patches of her hair had been pulled out traumatically. The victim had also suffered injuries caused by a blunt trauma to the mouth. There was evidence of forceful pinching and grabbing and human adult bite marks on the victim's body. The victim had suffered a blunt trauma to her pubic area. The forensic pathologist, found bruises in the forms of grab marks, belt marks, shoe marks, and marks from a radio antenna and a metal tray. The victim's brain was swollen with a hemorrhage both over the surface of the brain in the lining as well as a subdural hematoma between the skull bone and the brain. There were retinal hemorrhages in the back of her eyes indicating that she had been shaken violently. The Dr. opined that these injuries had been inflicted at various times, would have been painful, and would have required considerable force.

The resident family doctor at the Emergency Department, testified that he did not believe the victim's injuries were caused by a dog, but instead by "some sort of a beating." The Dr. testified that, based on their observations and on the history given to them by defendant, they believed that the victim had "been severely abused over a matter of days to weeks." A registered nurse in the Regional emergency room, opined, based on their experience and their observations of the victim's injuries, that the victim "had been beaten." The M.D., an expert in pediatric medicine who saw the victim in the pediatric intensive care unit at the Hospital, testified that, in their opinion, the victim was "a victim of severe child abuse." They concluded that the victim was a victim of the shaken-baby syndrome and the battered-child syndrome. The Dr. testified that, in his opinion, the victim's injuries were not caused by a dog, that the injuries were inflicted at various times, and that the victim was a victim of battered-child syndrome.

1998

The particulars in these crimes that the defendant and her co-defendant in a six-month time committed the offenses of first-degree burglary and 56 counts of breaking and entering/larceny after the fact and possession of stolen goods. The defendant and co-defendant broke in several apartments and trailers in different counties. The items taken were mostly sold or traded to obtain crack cocaine. The defendant would drive her car to different places, break in and bring the items out. The defendant pled guilty to one count of first-degree burglary and 56 counts of breaking and entering/larceny and possession of stolen goods and received a sentence of 103-133 months.

There was a different breed of inmates entering, young inmates (Millinneals) young, dumb, stupid and I don't care attitude. Upon inmates coming in as a new admission, revolving door inmates, they would have to receive PREA (Prison Rape Elimination Act) and some other training. PREA training was the most prominent. Inmates would receive information about this act, and it would go from 0-100 real fast. Inmates would report anything, everything was not considered PREA. In any case it had to be investigated, to rule it out. Let the investigations begin, it was not stop, along with all the other investigations, which were already in progress, soooo much paperwork. The OIC had the weight of the world on their shoulders. If there were 2 lieutenants there the same day, they would go back and forth, about who the OIC was. They would want to be the OIC, only if it was convenient for them, with no duties attached. Inmates calling PREA on staff or other inmates, to get them removed out of a certain area or placed under investigation, inmates using PREA to their advantage. I always felt that inmates making the allegations, should be removed to protect them from continued alleged acts that may occur. These inmates making allegations should receive disciplinary for these acts, should they turn out to be false. These investigations along with staff investigations, charging inmates, review incident reports. Most of the incident report came from our dining hall, inmate accident forms, if an inmate stump their toe and had to be seen by medical. Every accident report had to come with an incident report, out of all the reports that were done, they had to be reviewed and most were returned for corrections. We were lucky not to have reports missing because there were so many. Staff writing up inmates, you would have to go through them and see what should be processed or counseled. There were so many. I was told when I first started working that the ink pen is the most dangerous piece of equipment you have. If I didn't know how to do anything else, I knew how to write and summarize reports. Reports were a MONSTER at women's prison, but you learned and gained knowledge from it all.

I know there were some inmates I just wanted to slap the taste buds right out their mouth, just downright disrespectful, most of the time they had an audience. Once you take them out their element, most of the time they would calm down, to where you could actually talk to them. Then there were your Hispanic, latino and other groups, that you encounter, and they be talking that Spanish. Hell! I didn't know what they were saying, stating "no" speak English. REALLY!! They were the very ones that knew English very well, until they got in trouble and then it's "no speaka English." LOL I would say to them "no speaka Spanish." Later, you may walk up on them or by them and they seem to be speaking English very well, obviously they had forgot what they said.

Inmates have 24 hours a day 7 day a week to figure out how they could out smart staff and most of the time it worked because staff didn't pay attention. Staff was doing other things, like being on the telephone, instead of watching their surroundings. As a Correctional Officer you must remain vigilant in doing your job and be able to notice what we call RED flags. This was also critical, because you observe things out the ordinary, it was always your duty to report, no matter how small you think it is or if nothing came of it, you would have done your job. Since working in this environment, it has taught me a lot of thing, being observant, listen, know when to hold them and know when to fold them. I learned a great deal of things just having a wide range on watching and listening at what's going on around you at all times, don't let your guard down this is when things will happen. Inmates /people in general can be very unpredictable, a situation could go from 0-100 in a matter of seconds. You should know what to do to protect yourself.

We would get a call from the jail stating, they were transporting a very assaultive inmate and how long it would be before they arrive. We would go ahead and prepare with staff, have them in place to deal with the assaultive inmate, once they arrive. When the county arrives, the individual would be brought inside, but really not a problem. We prepare for the worse and hope for the best in the event there is a real problem with the admission being aggressive, assaultive or spitting.

2004

The county police were dispatched to a dead-end road to a shooting. Upon arriving at the scene, the police found the victim with lying face down with a gunshot wound to the head an another to his upper back. There were 3 spent shell casings and a small pocketknife near the victim's body. The victim was pronounced dead at the scene. The defendant and her mother were at the crime scene. The defendant told deputies that her and her mother was there for some land for sell, the victim followed them. The victim came up to the car and started cursing her. The defendant's mother got out the car to calm down the victim and the victim pulled a knife on her. He acted like he was going to charge her. The defendant who had her husband 9MM in the car shot in the air 2 times to scare the victim. The victim was still charging so the defendant shot him, and he fell to the ground. The victim was still trying to get up, so the defendant shot him again. The defendant does not remember how many shots were fired. The mother patted down the victim to see if he had a cell phone in his possession. The defendant stated that the victim had been wanting to have an affair with her and she would not do it. The defendant stated she "freaked out" and sat down until the police arrived. The defendant was charged with 2nd degree murder and her mother was charge with accessory after the fact.

1997

The defendant's grandmother age 81 was found dead in her bed, by the nursing home staff. The victims face was blotchy with red and brown colored spots, underneath the victim's head, the bed sheet had what appeared to be blood stains. The autopsy report indicated the pattern of petechial hemorrhages on the face, with sparing of the right cheek and chin areas. It is suggestive of something as a means of asphyxiation. However, hemorrhages within the tongue indicate that choking and or strangulation may have also played a role in the death. 1997 the defendant was found guilty of second-degree murder and sentenced to 189-236 months. Work release was not recommended.

7/15/15 @ 11:56 am Staff called a code blue on the radio. I heard staff radio for a stretcher, so I exited master control through the rear door towards the bicentennial yard, when I saw a staff running towards master control, stating "I need AED. In my mind I'm like oh Lawd the inmate's heart has stopped. I ran over to the area near the dining hall yard area and observed an inmate, who appeared to be giving another inmate mouth to mouth and this man. Upon me and the Sgt arriving the inmate and the male began to pick the inmate up. The man stated get her in the wheelchair! Get her in the wheelchair! I then started assisting with trying to get the inmate in the wheelchair. The inmate was partially in the wheelchair, as we were trying to transport, the chair hit a unlevel place in the sidewalk and the inmate's bottom half slide out the chair. I was trying to get her back in the chair and the man kept stating Go! Go! Go! As other staff arrived to assist with the transport, I just could not go further, my energy was gone, other staff continued with the transport, until they reached the medical unit with the inmate. Upon me reaching medical, staff moving quickly and was about to preform CPR. A miracle happen the inmate opened their eyes. The medical staff already knew the deal with this convict when we arrived. When the staff started preparing the inmate for the AED, the inmate listening to what was about to happen, they opened their eyes. So, it was all a ploy for the inmate's girlfriend to give her mouth to mouth in a sexual way. This man, which was some inmate advocate, I believe was a part of this ploy. I reported this incident to upper management, that myself along with other staff, could have been injured with this ploy, it was not a life or death situation.

1996

The defendant stated that her and her boyfriend went to the victim's house. The boyfriend was going to rob the victim and she was going to kill the victim. The victim had been known to loan people money and kept large amounts of cash on hand. The defendant stated that she had been to the residence before and given the victim oral sex. The victim was 84 years old. Once they arrived, she went inside the boyfriend stayed outside. After a few minutes, the boyfriend entered, and the victim ask how he was doing? The boyfriend replied, "don't ask me how the fuck I'm doing." The boyfriend told her to do what she had to do, or he would blow her head off. The victim began to walk towards the bedroom and the defendant raised the knife back and stated she could not do it and began to cry. Then they all began to tussle, the boyfriend pushes the knife into the victim, and he fell to the floor. The defendant then stabbed the victim herself. The boyfriend began beating her, took the knife from her, wrapped it in a towel and stabbed the victim twice more. The boyfriend took the victim's money. They then left the residence on foot. Shortly after leaving the boyfriend was picked up by a car, and she later got a ride home. Once the defendant arrived home, she washed her clothes and put them on the line to

dry. Later the victim was found lying in a pool of blood on the bedroom floor. The defendant pled guilty to 2nd degree murder and armed robbery. The defendant received 200-249 months for murder and 76-101 months in the armed robbery.

The mind set of an inmate especially, if they don't like you, is to do little irritating things and try to set you off to say or do something. 6/26/19 the Sgt received a call from staff in the dorm, who was extremely upset. Staff stated to the Sgt "you better come get this bitch, before I fuck them up." Upon arriving to the dorm, the staff stated, the inmate had taken their ink pen without permission. When staff told them to give the pen back, they exchanged words with the inmate. The inmate then took a marker, that was on their desk, as staff exited the office, the inmate threw the marker in the direction of the staff. The Sgt made contact with the inmate, who was in their room, placed them in handcuffs and escorted them out the building to the Sgts office.

There were several inmates, that came busting up in master control one time, being loud and disruptive something about the dining hall. I told them to "get the hell out of master control, coming up in here like you gone do something, get out!! When you calm down one of you can come back and explain what's going on. They were mad, but they got out. Later I took care of their issue. Inmates will push your buttons, and some knew how to do it well. I would just stand and stare at them and give them something to think about instead of entertaining their craziness. There have been many inmates that have tried me;

it takes different strokes for different folks. I always would tell people staff working at Women's Prison was not bad as they thought it was. Most women like to talk, this is how they cope. They are very talented as I'm sure the males are to. I've never worked at a male facility, so don't know much about that.

1989

A single mother charged with the grizzly death of her three toddler children, had appeared to be a nurturing parent who love the toddlers and had struggles feeding and sheltering them. The mother with a troubling past.

All three were had been stabbed multiple times when found in the home and the bodies dumped on the back porch of the neighbor's home. The neighbor wrestled with the 200-pound nude woman and tied her up before the authorities arrived.

The toddlers had hundreds of stab wounds, with a steak knife, had been disembowel and their organs strewn across the room where they were killed. The two older children were choked an eye of one child had been removed.

The Social workers learned that the mother had struggled to provide decent living for her children. A follow up report described the mother as caring mother whose children had an attachment and affection for her as she did them. The workers were shocked at the agency. This defies reason that someone can have a nurturing effect on children. Then all of a sudden this happens.

1989

The mother pled guilty and received 3 consecutive life sentences

Inmates are so slick; I work at this restaurant part time years ago. I went in one night and my boss man was telling me, how he had talked to one of the inmates, I was like how this could be. The inmate called collect of course and he wanted to know who was calling him from a correctional facility. They told me the inmate was trying to get them to send them some money. When they told me the name of the inmate, I was like Oh my God! How did they get this number to where I worked? I went back to work the next day investigating, talking to this inmate and of course they denied they called, which was a lie. I then put the fear of God in them, they told me they were in the office talking to a Lieutenant, saw the number on the desk and memorized it and called it when they returned to their dorm. Inmate stated yeah, I need some money. I see they was a businessman, maybe he would send me some money. I told that convict, if they ever call this number again, they would not like who I would become. This was a learning lesson to show you when you have inmates in your presence, in your office or anywhere that you have paperwork lying around, from the time they enter they are scanning your office, to see what they can pick up with their hands or eyes. Even if you are throwing away items, make sure they are destroyed or take them back home with you, because a few days later you may see them again and be like, I had one of those, how did the inmate get one like me? Da! The hands are always quicker than the eyes. You be standing there looking like Dumbo the fool, thinking you misplaced something, all the time the convict has swiped it.. Then staff will call you and say they confiscated some contraband from the inmate, that was just in your office or at your desk, the inmate states you gave them the item, a lie. Then some staff wouldn't even ask, because they would assume you gave it to them and it's ok. Inmates had a way of getting what they want; when they wanted it, most of the time they did, because there normally is 1 Officer. The inmate would tie them up with an issue or problem to keep them busy. If you were not smart enough to realize what they we doing, things would happen and you wouldn't even know until it was over.

Inmates would whoop each other's ass, you would not know anything until it was over or someone come tell it. Usually when inmates fight, they will disburse before staff arrive, so no one will not go to lock up. Inmates will come and tell you things after the fact, like well the fought all day yesterday. Sometimes the information would come to you and you would have to check it out, to see if it has any weight to it. Inmate allege they were going to beat another inmate with a lock in a sock. These are serious threats that have to be checked out. Inmates have cut other inmates with a razor and attempted to cut staff. That's why you always be mindful of your surroundings back, front and side, because you don't know the direction trouble may come.

2010

In a courthouse corridor swirling with television cameras, one family celebrated justice for its dead daughter. Another wept and cursed, helpless to rescue its daughter from life in prison. The man in the middle of a deadly love triangle was nowhere to be found. The boyfriend caused a perfect storm to happen and walked away from it," said Superior Court Judge, after a 12-member jury found his former mistress, guilty of killing his fiancée.

As the prosecution told the story, and as jurors apparently believed it, the defendant tried over and over to frame the former boyfriend for the murder of the victim, a graduate student at N.C. University, in January 2007.

Four months after the murder, police say, the defendant concocted a story in which the Ex forced her. Then left her in her Ford Explorer as he climbed to the second floor of the victim's apartment building, argued with her, shot her in the back of the head, ran back to the vehicle, shoved his handgun into his waistband, then hid in the back seat as she drove away.

A year later, authorities say, the defendant recorded fake telephone conversations and tried to pass them off as the Ex confessing to her. When that didn't convince investigators, the defendant falsely accused the Ex of raping her a year and a half after the murder.

In an emotional interview outside the courtroom Monday, the defendant's father again pointed the finger at the man who patrols the streets as a police officer.

"If it's the last thing I ever do, I will prove that he is the one who committed this murder," said the father, who with his wife sat for two weeks behind their daughter in a courtroom filled with loved ones seeking justice for the victim.

Hands shot up in jubilation when the verdict was announced, and heads nodded when he directed partial blame toward the Ex, who faces no charges in the crime.

After the trial, the officer answered his cell phone, the same phone whose records helped to clear him of the rape allegation. He declined to comment on the case.

The trial showed that the Ex made a habit of lying about his relationship with defendant to the victim, her family and police. But the jury decided the evidence pointed at the defendant, whose own lies struck closer to the heart of the case. She lied about driving there the day before the murder, about a gun she had bought a few months earlier, about a doctor's appointment on the morning of the murder and about whether she lived in the victim's apartment complex.

If the jury is right that the Ex's taped confessions were fake, that would be defendant biggest lie of all.

The defendant's attorney, tried to keep those tapes out of evidence, and when the judge allowed them, the defense attorney took them head-on, asking his client why her voice sounds strangely calm and the ex's voice sounds "more like Michael Jackson." The defendant said her former lawyers had told her to stay calm and try to get them to confess if he called her.

On Monday, the lawyer called for a mistrial after the jury asked to listen again to the tapes, even some they hadn't heard when Assistant District Attorney had introduced them into evidence last week. It was said the defendant had had access to the tapes for the past two years and could have addressed any portion of them during the trial.

In an impromptu news conference after the defendant's sentencing, her family insisted the confessions were real.

"My daughter, who is the perfect victim for someone like the ex, now has to spend the rest of her life in prison. The mother said.

As the defendant's family mourned the imprisonment of a daughter, sister and mother of two preteens, the victim's family felt a grim sense of justice.

"You took my baby away from me, and she wasn't yours to take," said the victim's mother. "There's no man worth anything like that. Someday, I may forgive you, but I don't. Right now, I hope you rot in hell. You're vile."

The defendant said nothing when the victim's mother gave her the chance.

The jury in the defendant's trial found her guilty of first-degree murder in the 2008 shooting of the graduate student. The judge immediately sentenced her to life in prison without parole. The defendant appeared stunned at the verdict. When the judge asked if she wanted to say anything, she sat silent. The victim's parents both addressed the defendant. "Because of what the defendant did there is a void. You took her away from me," said the mother. "Someday I may forgive you, but right now I don't, and I hope you rot in hell. You're vile. You don't deserve to be a mother."

During the trial, the defendant maintained her innocence, saying she did not shoot the victim and didn't even know the victim.

The jury began deliberating Friday. On Monday, the defense moved for a mistrial after jurors listened to phone calls that weren't introduced into evidence. According to the defense, that was grounds for a retrial. The judge denied the motion.

The jury continued listening to recorded calls Monday that were allegedly made by the victim's fiancé to the defendant.

The defendant and the victim were allegedly entangled in a love triangle with the police officer, who also was the victim's fiancé. Defense lawyers tried to pin the murder on the Ex - who denied involvement. The defendant testified on her behalf, telling the court she and the Ex were in a relationship, and she was pregnant with his child months before the murder but terminated the pregnancy. She also testified that on the morning of the murder, she accompanied the Ex and claimed that's when the Ex shot the victim outside her apartment. "If the last thing I ever do, I will prove that he is the one who actually committed that crime," the defendant's father said. "I won't rest, and I won't stop until he's where he belongs, in jail."

The defendant was a 911 operator at the time of the crime.

A jury on Monday found a former Metro 911 dispatcher guilty of killing a graduate student more than three years ago.

Jurors deliberated for about seven hours over two days before convicting the defendant of first-degree murder in the Jan. 4, 2007, shooting death of the victim.

"I was thankful to God for the guilty verdict because I was glad that she didn't get murdered twice," her father, said after the trial. "In my opinion, the evidence spoke for itself. It couldn't have been no other verdict but a guilty verdict."

Authorities maintained that the defendant stalked the victim in a jealous rage because she had a former relationship with the victim's fiancé, a police officer. The defendant contended that he stalked her and killed the victim. She said she feared him and did what he said only to protect her children from him. The father of the victim said he remains angry with man, who admitted during the trial that he dated the defendant and the victim at the same time. The father said he doesn't think he did enough to protect his daughter. He caused a perfect storm to happen and then walked away from it, and that was unfortunate for everyone in this case," The judge said as he sentenced the defendant.

There were a lot of inmates that appreciate the job you did, keeping order in your area. When certain staff came on duty, you could hear inmates boasting, "Let me see y'all do that shit you did last night." Inmates be like "yeah, I bet you get right now." When you work in a certain area for periods at a time, you know your inmates and they know you, how they act, whether they are in the right dorm, who your fighters are and the ones that got a whole lot of talk but no game. They will stand behind the next inmate, when the first blow is thrown. Inmates are famous for carrying a bone for another inmate to nibble on. I was told the inmates were going to fight, one of them was pregnant, the staff told the inmate "you are not going to fight her, she is pregnant", the inmate said "her face aint pregnant." WOW that was deep.

There were inmates that would leave cards for me, telling me how much they appreciate me. That goes along way, until they get in trouble, then we have to start all over again. This are some of the cards that, were left for me by inmates. Ms. Ford,

"Wow it' been a few years and I must say it has been an experience. Those few years ago this time, I would be upset with you right now because, I was still trying to find my way. You kept me grounded and refuse to give into what I wanted and not what I thought was best, for that I must say Thank You. A lot of people think living in this unit is a privilege, but honestly, it's a place that gives you time to mature and grow. I have grown so much and can understand so much more. I guess you see something in me that no one else did. I raised myself, never met my father and mother... but throughout the years you've been that supporting parent to whether you know it or not. From small lessons in life, to cleaning to death, or simply being at a play or program I put together. If you could adopt me, I'd let you. Thanks you'll never understand the effect you had on my life. Please don't ever stop grabbing our hands that's reaching out."

Capt. Ford

We wanted to take the time to wish you a Merry Christmas, but also know, you are greatly appreciated for everything you do. We can really truly say that your good people.It's hard sometimes being here for the holidays, but knowing we have someone like you to back us up and keep us straight, it keeps us going strong. So just know that you are cared about and greatly appreciated.

Ms. Ford,

You are an inspiration in my life. I really appreciate you. Thanks for everything Ms. Ford.

This is what made me love what I do and do what I love

I would always go by the moon, as to when the freaks would come out. If it was a full moon watch out, because it was going to be crazy, Its like the inmates would be watching the moon to. LOL! Inmates being transported outside hospital, especially pregnant inmates, sometimes they would go back to back, you still trying to make that turnip bleed red. Then a high-risk inmate would have to go out, that required a Sgt and 1,2,3 Officers and two vehicles, fight after fight, nowhere to lock up anyone. There was never a boring minute, if someone say they were bored could not highly be possible. It just seemed like some bad cycle, you would leave go home and return the next morning, it seemed like hell had broken a loose. There would be anywhere from 6-8 inmates out, which required at least two Officers and 7 staff call outs, inmates at 3 different hospital. What do you do? You make it work somehow, it had to be done. You start sending supervisors because, you have exhausted other avenues. Decisions had to be made at the drop of a hat, you had to be confident in your decision making and stand behind your decision.

1999

Police was dispatched to a shooting. Upon arrival, the victim had already been transported to the hospital. The officers entered and secured the crime scene. There was a substantial amount of blood and some brain matter on the couch. A shot gun was propped against the wall. It was later found out that the gun was used to shoot at the suspects' car as they sped away. Several people had gone to the victim's house to hang out to drink and smoke weed. While there two of the suspects got into a fight with another individual. When 1 of the suspects boyfriends returned, they left and returned to their home and picked up another person and returned to the apartment. One of the suspects was carrying a tire iron in her hand. They inquired about someone that had left. At this time a guy got between them with a shot gun in his hand and shouted, "give it up." Everyone emptied their pockets and threw their money on the floor. The victim was standing in front of the suspects when they ask why he was running his mouth to their boyfriend. The suspect pulled back the tire iron to strike the victim when the victim held up his arm and leg to stop the blow. Soon the suspect stepped in and shot the victim, some of the victim's head fell off on the couch, the suspects then picked up the money from the floor and fled. Upon an investigation being conducted and police arrival at the apartment a male was standing outside. When the suspect observed the police, he went back inside and barricaded the door. SWAT arrived to assist. The suspects surrendered and was taking into custody and later identified by photo lineup. The victims were able to identify who committed the crime and shot and killed the victim. The suspects were arrested and charged with murder.

1998

Two suspects decided they would rob the victim because he was a big-time drug dealer. The victim was found on the bed on his knees shot in the back. The suspects did carry away the personal property of the victim including a safe with a unknown amount of currency. The suspect committed these acts by means of assault and possessing a firearm. The suspect threatens and endangered this the life of the victim in concert with the other suspect.

1977

On April 1978 the suspect entered a guilty plea to murder in the second-degree robbery with a dangerous weapon. After accepting her plea the court sentenced the defendant to the full term of Natural Life. Recommending the defendant never be paroled. Sentenced to 50 years in prison. The defendant and her Co-defendants had been riding around drinking and doing drugs, went to the victim's home Upon the defendants arriving at the victim's home. The victim opened the front door and was confronted by a pointed pistol. Upon entering the house other people were awaken arguments and shout began. One of the victims seemed confused about what was going on. During the events two of the suspects brought gasoline into the house. The suspect began to threaten another victim with a knife. The gasoline was poured onto the floor of the house. One of the suspect's started shooting the victims in the house. One defendant struck a match to the gasoline which had been poured on the floor. The suspects left immediately, got into their car and drove off. The victim was able to remove himself and other victims except one that he was unable to get out, because the fire had completely consumed the house.

2006

Three case of felony trafficking with intent to sell and deliver. The subject sold $2500.00 with of Cocaine to an undercover officer. The defendant was arrested when she tried to attempt another sale.

I always had staff that did not like me for whatever reason. I never let that stop me from doing my job. I was summoned to the Warden's office, they were telling me that staff was filing a grievance on me, I'm like ok, when they told me who the staff was, I was shocked, because the staff was new. They have never approached me or even had a conversation with me, but I intimidated them WHAT!! There was staff that claim I was harassing them just to get move to the rotation they wanted. There was a supervisor that always kept some shit stirred up. They would tell a lie and you be literally standing right there looking them in the face. I had informed them that I would yank their chain when it was necessary, to keep them in line. They in turn when an stated that I was harassing them, to get moved to the opposite rotation, which was what they wanted. I was glad because I didn't have time to baby sit a grown person and their actions, let someone else deal with them.

There was no room in my duties to micromanage grown people. I came in one morning, the Sgt was not in the office, so I left them a note, about inmate identification board. Well later, the Sgt called me asking, what they were supposed to advise maintenance about the board. I ask them "why were they calling me, why they did not know what was going on." I told them I would be up there in a few minutes. I proceeded to the area and informed maintenance what I needed; it was not a problem. I walked into the conference room and found a torn mattress lying on the floor. I informed the Sgt that the mattress needs to be moved out of the area. I returned to my office. The Sgt followed me and stated, I got something on my mind, and we need to talk. The Sgt stated I feel like you have something personal against me, whatever I do is not right, I have dropped everything, I was doing to do what you ask me to do." I informed the Sgt, I don't do personal at work I do my job. I expected them to do their job as a Sgt as well. I don't have time to micromanage them. I expect them to be responsible of their duties, the same way they expect their Officers, to step up to the plate, they need to do the same. I have given instructions for them to complete a task, which I should not have to do. I gave them a task to move fans in the AM, that afternoon the task had still not been completed. They told me that it had been handled. I informed them Yes! It has been done because I took care of it. Well everyone wants a pat on the back. I expect all Sgt to do their jobs and be responsible. You can't adjust your line up in the mornings for staff call outs, if you don't check in with the OIC. When staff from 6p is not relieved on time, staff will be upset because, someone was relieved that was late and they reported for duty on time. Just like you, if you don't get relief, you are going to call all the roosters and hens, so you can get out on time. So, you treat your staff the way you want to be treated. I was standing on the yard talking to an inmate, the Sgt exited the dorm, coming across the grounds towards me stating "hey you the one I want to see." I been looking for you," being very disrespectful. I turned and look at them, because I thought they were talking to an inmate. I ask "who you talking to, you are not going to talk to me any kind of way. I know you ain't talking to me." Then the assistant Unit Manager walked up. The Sgt began to tell me that they had moved a fan from one dorm to another that already had their limit fans. So, my asst. states, I told them to move the fan and put there, because inmate stated she was not getting any air. The Sgt stated, "well you know this inmate is sickly." I ask them were they going to be able to give, all the inmates a personal fan. There are a lot of inmates, that have medical issues, will you be able to accommodate them to. I told them when an issue arises about the fan, I will direct the inmates to you. I then proceeded to my office. I would come in for duty in the mornings and the Sgt would standing out on the grounds talking to staff and the unit grounds were a disaster. The grounds are to be cleaned daily, all day. I could not get them to understand this concept. I continuously explained, there were to many inmates with extra duty from disciplinary, unassigned inmates with no job assignment, Hell, there were even inmates that would volunteer just to have something to do. There were absolutely no excuses for the unit grounds to be out of order. Later, my assistant tried to check me, about the Sgt stating, I could have called them aside, out the sight of the inmates. I could see you fussing, shaking and moving your head. I sure did, because you are not going to approach me in a disrespectful manner and not get corrected. I was talking to an inmate, other inmates waiting to talk to me. I informed my assistant that, they could allow the Sgt to address them any kind of way. I will let out my bag of tricks and in turn they may not like how they are treated or spoken to. The Sgt approached me wrong and I reacted. It may not have been right in your eyes, but I betcha it won't happen again. Always have to watch out for those **Lions, Tigers and Bears.**

2002

Just after 3:30 in the morning, 911 operators received a frantic call.

"I need an ambulance. I need an ambulance here — I need the police here — NOW," she can be heard saying on phone recordings. "Somebody killed my husband while we were sleeping... somebody shot him."

When first responders arrived at the home, the caller met them outside and said she had been awoken by a gunshot and saw someone standing over her husband. After another gunshot, the supposed intruder ran off into the night. According to the prosecutor, those at the scene described her as "not overly distraught, not tearful or anything like that. Inside the home, investigators found the victim lying in bed with fatal gunshot wounds to his head and chest. Also, home asleep at the time were the two young boys, their half-sister and a friend, who was sleeping over.

Despite her claims that she was in bed with the victim at the time of his murder, she didn't appear to have any blood on her. There were also no signs of a break-in and no items missing from the residence. Police brought the caller, her daughter

166

and friend down to the station for gunshot residue tests. The daughter and the friend were clean, but she tested positive. The pattern of the gunshot residue, however, revealed she was not the shooter. With nothing to hold them on, they were allowed to leave.

While searching their home in the aftermath of the shooting, police found an extensive pornography collection underneath the bed. On the victim's computer, they also found homemade pornographic photographs. According to the prosecutor, the photos included "about four men and a female" and they were "engaged in sexual intercourse and positions and two at one time and things like that." The woman in the photographs was the caller, while the men included her husband and family friend.

After being brought in for questioning, the friend told police he met the victim and the caller in an online chat room. They invited him to join the "Gang Bangers," a "swingers" club that held monthly sex parties. At one party, the friend had sex with the caller and another woman. On another occasion, he and victim had sex with the caller at the same time.

The caller and the friend eventually began seeing each other outside of the sex party circuit. This upset victim.

The victim became concerned about how much she was seeing the friend." said a prosecutor. "It was becoming more than someone that she was having a sexual relationship with." The caller told the friend she was in love with him.

The friend later testified, "I'd tell her what she wanted to hear to get what's at the end of the rainbow, which was to get her to co-sign for my motorcycle."

Despite his salacious tales of the sexual exploits, the friend wasn't a suspect in the victim's murder. The Police Department, however, soon received an anonymous phone calling saying the daughter was the killer. Not only that, but the caller also said she killed her stepfather on the orders of her mother.

Police interviewed the only person in the home the night of the killing who wasn't a family member. A prosecutor told "Snapped:" "The Detective went and found the female friend, brought her in for an interview and at that point, somewhat cracked and told what she knew."

When police arrested the caller, her 15-year-old daughter was nowhere to be found. A couple days later, police found the daughter hiding under a bed in a trailer owned by one of her friends. Both mother and daughter were charged with the same crimes; first-degree murder and conspiracy to murder.

When questioned by police, the tough-talking teenager quickly offered up her mother on a plate. An investigator told "Snapped" that she "broke down and told me the facts."

According to the daughter, the mother wanted the victim out of the way so she could be with the friend. Prosecutors thought the victim's $700,000 life insurance policy and military benefits had something to do with it as well. The District Attorney's office offered the daughter a reduced sentence if she agreed to testify against her mother.

The prosecution's star witness was 15-year-old killer the daughter. She told the jury her mother asked her to find someone to kill her stepfather and then pressured her into pulling the trigger herself when she couldn't find a hitman. The tawdry sex life was on full display during the trial, with the couple's homemade pornography shown in court. The mother refused to take the stand in her own defense.

At the trial's conclusion, the mother was found guilty on all counts and sentenced to life in prison without parole. As part of her deal with prosecutors, the daughter received a maximum sentence of 31-and-a half years. The victim's family stood by the mother, laying blame solely at the daughter's feet.

"The daughter is a very vindictive, evil child the victim's sister later told "Snapped," "I know the mother is innocent, she had nothing to do with the victim's murder. This was the daughter's evilness."

Now 50, the mother is serving out her life sentence quietly. The daughter now 30 years old, earliest possible release date is in 2029, when she will be 42 years old.

YEAR 1999

The defendant committed the act of 2nd degree murder and robbery with a dangerous weapon. While living in the area, the defendant met her co-defendant who also live in the same area. The co-defendant moved in an apartment with a friend. Around this time the victim had received an inheritance in the excess $100.000.00 and moved into the apartment complex. The co-defendant moved into the victim's apartment to reside. The victim's family had not been in contact with her. The victim's family reported her missing after she failed to come to a family birthday party. The family member met with the police department investigator. The investigator and the family member went to the victim's apartment to look around. The investigation of the apartment revealed a large amount of blood on the sofa in the living room and traces of blood in surrounding areas. There was evidence that efforts were made to clean up the crime scene. It appears the victim was moved from the sofa and placed in a duffel type gold bag, that was placed on the floor at the foot of the bed and covered with bedding and clothing items. As the investigator looked around the apartment, they noticed an odor and moved some items from the duffel bag and discovered what was believed to be the body of the victim. According to a friend of the victim and the co-defendant, the co-defendant knew the victim's pin number to the victim's ATM card. Bank records show repeated activity on the ATM card. The last transaction was in another state. The victim's green Mazda was also missing. The defendant and the co-defendant were last seen in the victim's car. The defendants were later apprehended in another state. The victim was asleep on the couch when the defendant came to visit the co-defendant. While at the apartment the defendants covered the victim's head with a pillow and beat the victim repeatedly with a hammer. The victim died from blunt force trauma to the head.

1991

This suspect was asked about a large amount of money seized at her home in another state. The suspect stated that the money belonged to a big-time drug dealer. The drug dealer had agreed to pay her for keeping the money. The subject stated she was in prison for about 5 months for this when the money was found. Then the subject says she was approach again about transporting cocaine to NC for him. The subject stated she transported 3 kilograms, she remained in the hotel 4 days while the drug dealer went out and conducted his business. The subject was contacted again about transporting 3 kilograms of cocaine, which was in her luggage. The subject stated she stayed in the room until the drugs were sold, she met no one. After 6 days alone, she left. This continue several more times, until she was arrested and agreed to cooperate because she knew she needed help. The defendant pled guilty and was found guilty with conspiracy to traffic in cocaine, traffic in possession, traffic by transportation. The defendant received 25 years for each charge.

2001

On December 9, 2001, the defendant called an emergency line to report that he had just found the victim unconscious in their mansion and suspected she had fallen down "fifteen, twenty, I don't know" stairs. He later claimed that he had been outside by the pool and had come in at 2:40 am to find the victim at the foot of the stairs. The defendant said she must have fallen down the stairs after consuming alcohol and Valium.

Toxicology results showed that the victim's blood alcohol content was 0.07 percent). The autopsy report concluded that the 48-year-old victim sustained a matrix of severe injuries, including a fracture of the thyroid neck cartilage and seven lacerations to the top and back of her head, consistent with blows from a blunt object, and had died from blood loss ninety minutes to two hours after sustaining the injuries. The victim's daughter and the victim's sister, both initially proclaimed the defendant's innocence and publicly supported him alongside his children, but the sister reconsidered after learning of the defendants bisexuality, as did the daughter after reading her mother's autopsy report. Both subsequently broke off from the rest of the family.

Although forensic expert, hired by the defendant's defense, testified that the blood-spatter evidence was consistent with an accidental fall down the stairs, police investigators concluded that the injuries were inconsistent with such an accident. As the defendant was the only person at the residence at the time of the victim's death, he was the prime suspect and was soon charged with her murder. He pleaded not guilty.

The medical examiner concluded that the victim had died from lacerations of the scalp caused by a homicidal assault. There were total of seven lacerations to the top and back of the victim's head were the result of repeated blows with a light, yet rigid, weapon. The defense disputed this theory. According to their analysis, the victim's skull had not been fractured by the blows, nor was she brain damaged, which was inconsistent with injuries sustained in a beating death.

The trial drew increasing media attention as details of the defendant's private life emerged. The prosecution team attacked the defendant's credibility, focusing on his alleged misreporting of his military service and what they described as a "gay life" he led and kept secret. The prosecution contended that the defendant's marriage was far from happy, suggesting that the victim had discovered the defendant's alleged secret "gay life" and wanted to end their marriage. It was the main motive that the prosecution offered at trial for the victim's alleged murder (the other being a $1.5 million life insurance policy). According to Assistant District Attorney.

The victim would have been infuriated by learning that her husband, who she truly loved, was bi-sexual and having an extramarital relationship—not with another woman—but a man, which would have been humiliating and embarrassing to her. We believe that once she learned this information that an argument ensued, and a homicide occurred. The defense argued that the victim accepted the defendant's bisexuality and that the marriage was very happy, a position supported by their children and other friends and associates.

The prosecution said that the victim's murder was most likely committed with a custom-made fireplace poker called a blow poke. It had been a gift to the defendant from the victim's sister but was missing from the house at the time of the investigation. Late in the trial the defense team produced the missing blow poke, which they said had been overlooked in the garage by police investigators. Forensic tests revealed that it had been untouched and unmoved for too long to have been used in the murder. A juror contacted after the trial noted that the jury dismissed the idea of the blow poke as the murder weapon.

Verdict

On October 10, 2003, after one of the longest trials in North Carolina history, a jury found the defendant guilty of the murder of the victim and he was sentenced to life in prison without the possibility of parole. Denial of parole requires premeditation. Despite the jury accepting the murder was a "spur-of-the-moment" crime, they also found it was premeditated. As one juror explained it, premeditated meant not only planning hours or days ahead, but could also mean planning in the seconds before committing a spur-of-the-moment crime. The defendant was released on December 16, 2011.

Owl theory

In late 2009, a new theory of victim's death was raised: that she had been attacked by an owl outside, fallen after rushing inside, and been knocked unconscious after hitting her head on the first tread of the stairs. The police were approached by a neighbor suggesting an owl might have been responsible, after reading the evidence list and finding a "feather" listed. The defendant's attorneys had determined that the crime lab report listed a microscopic owl feather and a wooden sliver from a tree limb entangled in a clump of hair that had been pulled out by the roots found clutched in the victim's left hand. A re-examination of the hair in September 2008 had found two more microscopic owl feathers. The jury been presented with this evidence it would have "materially affected their deliberation and therefore would have materially affected their ultimate verdict". A new motion was filed in August 2010 one of the defendant's original attorneys, who acted *pro bono* in proceedings challenging the crime lab testimony.

On December 16, 2011, the defendant was released from the county jail on $300,000 bail and placed under house arrest with a tracking anklet. His release on bond followed a judicial order for a new trial after it was found that the crime lab had given "materially misleading" and "deliberately false" testimony about bloodstain evidence, and had exaggerated his training, experience, and expertise. Alford plea. A movie STAIRCASE (several other televised productions)

As a OIC you had to deal with everything, everyone, staff, medical and the inmates. I had a supervisor call me and state they were having a problem with an employee refusing their job assignment and another employee that had already worked 12 hours went to complete the task of dispensing medication to the inmates. I proceeded to the area and talked with the employee. I stated "I was understanding that they were refusing their work assignment. I informed them, I was there so they could gather their belongings and I would be escorting them out of the facility. They were not to return to work until Monday to talk to management. They seem shocked stunned and amazed at what was coming out of my mouth. I ask again are you refusing your work assignment? They stated "yes, it's too much." I then stated, "due to you refusing your assignment and being insubordinate, they were being relieved of their duties and being escorted out the facility." They stated, "I been doing this for 35 years." I stated oh so you can retire? I explained to them, because you have 35 years, does not mean you can refuse your assignment on a job and be insubordinate to your supervisors, do what you wanna do." They stated "I have gone to my supervisors and nothing was done. I will not lose my license because I made a mistake doing my job." I ask why would they lose their job.? They stated "from walking back and forth to my assigned area, which was only about 100 yards. I then ask "have you ever been down to the units, all the way down the hill, that's a WALK!! I then advised them to talk to management with their problems and concerns. This was not the way to handle the problem and you look like a reasonable individual. Well by time the conversation ended, they agreed to continue with their assignment, which had already been completed, by someone else and it only took 20 mins.

9/1/07 The Lt. 2nd shift OIC was informed by the control desk officer, that a phone call was received from someone identifying themselves as a staff sister. The caller was advised that the OIC was unavailable. The caller proceeded to state that, the staff and another sister were involved in an automobile accident and the staff would not be able to report for duty. The Officer stated it sound like the call was made from a cell phone, due to static and echo in the line, someone sounding like the staff, telling the caller what unit and shift they worked. The caller was informed that the staff must call back and talk to the OIC. The information was provided to the OIC upon their availability. The next day talking with the staff, they stated they did not recall the reason they did not report for duty. It was a possibility; they did not have a babysitter. The reason they have been late so many times was because they did not have a car. Staff stated they will no longer have that problem, because they have a car and their children have a new babysitter at night. This staff has been placed on 3 action plans and time management all of which was violated. This was a constant problem with staff not showing up, being late or calling in creating problems for the institution being short staff. The process to deal with these individuals was slow or nothing happen at all. This has been a continued problem throughout my career. These were staff you could not get rid of, for whatever reasons, it had a lot to do with their morals. You would provide the appropriate paperwork; it was always something wrong with it and it had to be sent back for more information. Well by time you put in the leg work, time, to provide what is needed, the paperwork was too old or you had to do away with it and start all over. JUST TOO MUCH!!!!

7/11/09 Staff reported to the OIC that master control received a telephone call from an outside caller, requesting to speak to a staff. The Officer informed the caller that the staff was not at the facility and did not work this rotation. The caller then stated that the staff was at work, because they had just received a text message stating they were in the dorm. The OIC contacted the Sgt in the unit by telephone instructing them to have the staff relieved and escort them to master control with their belongings. Once in operation conference room the Capt began questioning the staff concerning possession of a cell phone, while within the confinements of the institution. The staff stated, they had a cell phone in their possession and sent a text to their family member in another state. The staff further stated that they had called their other family member in another state. The Capt then ask for the phone, which the staff retrieved from their food bag and turned it over to the Capt. Upon the Capt receiving the phone it was already on. The Capt opened the phone and it was revealing that it was operating in silent mode. The phone was a sprint Sanyo with camera capabilities. The capt then entered the text message feature, which revealed a message was sent "call me at work, in the dorm" with a call back number, which was registered to the phone. The Capt then entered the call feature to reveal the time the call was placed to the staff other family member. Then the picture feature was accessed to reveal pictures of the family sent to the staff phone. When attempting to open the pictures, it could not be opened due to the service plan. There were no pictures of the inmates or the facility within. The phone was then turned off, returned to the staff and the staff was instructed to return the phone back to their vehicle with the Sgt to ensure that it was done. Management was notified. The staff was allowed to return back to their assigned post and dorm.

6/25/10 Social worker III reported that an inmate whose work assignment is MATCH delivers documents back and forth to the Social work Staff, entered the dorm to deliver documents to another Social Worker. When the staff who was assigned to the dorm questioned the inmate, why was they in their building? The inmate stated to deliver some documents to the Social Worker. When the inmate attempted to show the staff their pass the staff turned and walk away stating "what's really your job description? The inmate then asks the staff to call the Social Worker that sent them. The inmate then began to explain their job duties. The staff stated to the inmate "you think you somebody." The inmate became very upset and went to another dorm to talk to another staff. The inmate returned to the Programs building and reported the incident to the Social Worker. The Social Worker called the staff and informed them that the inmate works for programs. The SW states the staff immediately became defensive, talking about staff letting inmates get away with things they should not have, like chemicals and mop heads. The SW stopped staff by stating "I didn't know what they were talking about. I only want to address the issue a hand. Staff then became belligerent and accused the SW of taking the inmate's side. Staff stated to the SW, that they were following policy. The inmate throws their name around and thinks that it is going to get them special favors. The SW stated to staff "that no one has ever complained about the inmate to me in the past," before they could finish their statement, staff stated "oh, so you are sticking up for the inmate." The SW stated "I see I'm not getting anywhere with you, because you have an attitude. The Social Worker reported "I ended the conversation, because I could see the staff was very angry. "I was not going to get into a shouting match with them, when the inmate has a pass to enter the dorm to deliver a package, to the other Social Worker.

11/21/10 in the Unit Sgts office 2 staff became in involved in a verbal confrontation, with each other. During the confrontation, both staff was using profane language being unprofessional towards each other. Referring to each other as bitches and mother fuckers, failing several directives given by supervisors to cease the madness, which resulted in the supervisor, stepping between the staff to separate them. Staff stated to the supervisor "I would like to apologize for my behavior and stated it will not happen again. "Staff proceeded to walk towards the dorm where another supervisor and staff was standing. The staff ask the other staff, can I speak to you, as they walk to the office behind the supervisor. The other staff threw a attitude and said "no." Staff then ask the other staff to come to the office. The supervisor then called the staff to the office. While proceeding to the office the staff began running their mouth. Upon entering the office, staff asked the other staff "what is wrong." Why there is so much beef between them?" Staff replied stating "I squashed it, by not saying anything to you," not saying it directly at me, but sitting around in front of me, referring to me as a bitch or that bitch, really mean you squashed it." Staff then went back and forth for about 2 or 3 mins, arguing about the situation. The staff stated they were not violent or at any time want to strike the other staff. Only thing they wanted to do was solve the situation. "It's not about being emotional or that I worry what people say. It's about coming to work and staff not responding to a radio call, asking for relief, to get food and the Staff throwing an attitude with you, calling that staff post, when they working, to inform them of changes, that going to affect their dorm and they hang up on you. When attitudes affect your job performance, that's when it becomes a problem. I have been dealing with that attitude. My Supervisor is also aware of the situation. If I could I would like to be moved to another rotation."

JULY 3, 2001

The evidence presented at trial tended to show the following: in the fall of 1996, the 30-year old defendant went regularly to the home of 84-year old victim, she knew where the victim kept her money and when the victim's monthly checks arrived, and she told her friend that she was "getting" money from victim and she told her friend, "I ought to rob her, hit that bitch in the head."

Defendant indicated in a statement to police that, on 10 December 1996, she went to the victim's home to pay back some money she owed her. Defendant asked to borrow more money, but the victim said no. Defendant then went to use the phone in victim's bedroom, opened her dresser drawer when the victim wasn't looking, and removed $10.00. The victim "caught" defendant taking the money and demanded it back. She allegedly grabbed defendant's coat sleeve and pushed her, and defendant pushed her back. Defendant maintained that the victim then hit a closet door and grabbed some plastic bags as she fell to the floor. The bags purportedly "caught on [the victim's] face" and she struggled to remove them. Defendant claimed she began putting more bags on the victim, and the victim started wheezing. It appeared to defendant the victim had gotten part of a bag in her mouth, and the victim asked defendant to help her, but defendant "was scared and couldn't move." "I just watched her choke herself . from the bags being over her face that she just couldn't get off alone." Defendant hoping the victim essentially "killed herself from fighting herself with the plastic bags."

On 11 December, law enforcement officers discovered the victim's body lying at the front door inside her home. The victim had been dead for a number of hours, and her body was fully clothed and lying face up with a brown plastic grocery bag pressed tightly around her neck. Newspapers and five or six plastic grocery bags were in disarray around the immediate area of her body. There was no evidence of a struggle anywhere else in the home. The autopsy showed the victim had eight broken ribs and a depression in the skin around most of her neck. The cause of death was a combination of ligature strangulation (strangulation with a device pulled around the neck) and smothering.

Defendant was subsequently indicted for armed robbery and murder. The jury found her guilty of common law robbery and first-degree murder under the theory of felony murder, with robbery as the underlying felony. The jury was unable to reach a unanimous verdict with regard to awarding defendant the death penalty. The trial court arrested judgment on the robbery conviction and sentenced defendant to life in prison without parole. Defendant appealed to this Court.

5/1/15 Good staff burnt out, due to staff shortages, staff fail to report for duty when scheduled, morale was low, staff disrespectful towards supervisors. Sgts disrespectful to staff and their peers. They base their working relationship on likes and dislikes, no work ethics. Personal and professional relationships should be kept separate. If not you should only have a professional work relationship. Sgts can't make simple decisions and don't want responsibilities that the position carries. You have staff walking around with stripes. Supervisors cannot reprimand their staff, when you are doing the same or worse than your subordinate.

9/19/11 My Lt. informed me that the staff had come to them and requested to be off on Friday. I informed the Lt. that was up to them, would they be able to afford the staff to be off. The Lt. informed me the staff could be off, but to report for duty at 12:00 pm. So I ask the Lt. Why they didn't come to me. Later, that day the staff entered the office and the Lt. stated "well there she is right there, go ahead and ask her. The staff stated No! you suppose to ask. I exited the office and continued my duties. I had no idea what those two were discussing prior to. On 9/23/11 The staff entered the facility along with myself, my supervisor and several other staff. As we were standing in master control near the microwave, the staff walked through and spoke to my supervisor by name.

I had entered the OIC office where the Lt. and staff were having a conversation about line up, because the staff did not like what the Lt. said. The staff took an attitude, got loud with the Lt. and stormed out the office. I then informed the Lt. do not allow the staff. to conduct themselves that way toward them and you not respond. I directed them to get that staff back in here, and address them about their conduct. The Lt. called the staff in to talk with them, as I remained outside, the door at master control. The staff became loud a couple of times during the meeting. I looked through the OIC window of the door. The staff became loud again, I then entered the office. I ask them what was wrong with them, as they sit there crying and snotting, stating that the Capt./Lt. we're mistreating them yelling at them. I stated to the staff, it's ok for you to do what you do, but when the shoes are on the other feet you can't take it or come up with you being mistreated. I stated to the staff. I knew it was not going to be long, before your mood hit you, because of the way they were acting. The staff then went back to line up a whole week ago, stating "You cut me off in line up and people were laughing at me." This was an issue we had previously discussed, and they were still carrying it around. Then the staff became loud stating "MOVE me! MOVE me! I explained to them, "I don't have the authority to move you. I ask the staff, If you have something you need to say to me, then you need to say it, so we can move on, instead of spinning your wheels in the same mud hole, as the staff was sitting in the chair by the closet door. I get up and make a ½ step towards them and they stated "you going to walk up on me. "I inform them I knew them very well; I did not have time to play games. They always use, we are mistreating them, when they are called out on something they have done.

I had staff to enter the supervisor office, go into the file drawer, that should have be lock and remove their file. The staff approached me stating, they need to discuss their file with me. I explain to them, you have no authority to come in this office and remove anything, especially a TAP. They were informed they need to return the file back to the file drawer. I removed the file from their hand and placed it back in the drawer. I guessed they thought they intimidated me, NOT!!! However, it was nothing wrong with them seeing their file, there is a way to do it. You just don't go in an office, go through files because you think you can. I had previously talked to the Supervisors and told them if they were not in the office, the door should be secured. The HANDS are quicker than the EYES.

1725 6 pm shift arriving for relief. I told the Lt. and staff we could finish the conversation in the Capts office. The staff and I entered my office. I told them this was not about work. This is about something else, if they did not want to talk to me they had several options. I informed them they needed to talk to someone, because whatever it was, it's effecting your job performance. I told them I did not know what else to do to help you. The staff stated no one can help me, no one can help me. The Lt. ask the staff what's wrong? Talk to us. There was silence and the staff ask could they leave. That was the end of that.

SNAPPED 2007

The defendant in this case avoided a sentence of life without parole Monday by pleading guilty to second-degree murder and first-degree kidnapping in Brunswick County Superior Court.

The defendant, was sentenced by Special Superior Court Judge to between about 22 1/2 years and 28 1/2 years in prison. The Bolivia woman had initially been charged with first-degree murder in connection with the Sept. 5 shooting death of the victim, was shot in the parking lot of the former Restaurant, off N.C. 211, west of Supply.

The defendant initially told authorities she had driven Bussard to meet a man at the intersection of N.C. 211 and N.C. 214 to pick up a car. She eventually confessed to shooting the victim twice in the head. The defendant may have been involved with the victim's estranged husband, court officials said.

The victim's mother, offered a victim impact statement before the defendant was sentenced.

"She just talked about what a good person her the defendant was. She had a lot of friends. The mother indicated she didn't harbor any malice toward the defendant. She wants to move on with her life," Assistant District Attorney said.

The N.C. Capital Defender's Office became involved in the defendant's defense because of the possibility of capital punishment being sought.

The plea agreement was acceptable to all parties involved in the case, "We feel like under the circumstances it worked out pretty good for everybody. "It brought closure to the victim's family and it got defendant out of the situation she was in - life without parole.

After the shooting, the defendant described a name to investigators as a tall, slender man, who wore his blond hair in a ponytail and had a "scraggly" goatee.

She even helped an artist produce a composite sketch before admitting her role in the crime.

The defendant volunteered with the County rescue squad and worked as a medical technician for a local company.

The victim, an Alabama native, had left work at the Restaurant before the shooting.

The victim also worked as a bartender at several other bars in the area.

The decision to offer a second-degree murder plea to the defendant was not made lightly.

"We had to think long and hard about whether to take the plea.

"This was what the victim's family indicated they wanted us to do the defendant will be in prison until her mid-60s."

5/10/12 I contacted the Lt. Eagle housing about some paperwork, that I presented to them for an officer. The Lt. stated "well you need to correct the paperwork, because it was another Lt. name on it. I told them, once they were done with getting with the staff, get it back to me, I could make corrections. Upon the Lt. bringing the paperwork back, there were statements missing. I called and ask for the statements that were not in there4/3,22/12 and the action plan that was open in April 2011. They sent 2011 which was the incorrect paperwork. I called and ask again, and they sent, and they sent the action plan and the other 2 statements originally in packet that I sent to them. Once I prepared the paperwork over, I called for the Officer to come to master control. Upon talking with them and informing them that I was advising them of an internal investigation, they acted surprised and ask why? I informed them due to their lateness and call outs. They stated to me "that's already been taken care of." I ask them what they meant, they informed me they had receive an action plan from their Lt. Then the Lt. walk in and ask the staff to step out. I ask the Lt. did they give the staff an action plan and they stated "yes.". The one they had was from last year and could not be used. I informed them "yes", but they violated it. I had talked to them on several occasions, trying to give them a chance. The Lt. ask me why? I did not send the paperwork to them. I informed them, that I did not want to leave them out the loop. The Lt. stated "it ain't about leaving us out the loop, the Sgts need to do their job!!! You should not be doing this." I informed them that, I was aware of this, but at the same time when I came to this rotation, I had a demand for control of the shift, because there was not any. So Yes, I took the job on of doing what needed to be done, because there was no control. The Lt. began telling me, what they did on 3rd shift. I told them "fine you do that in your area of EHU and you can TAP your staff for not doing their job. I will not allow the work I am putting into getting this rotation on the right track, go by the wayside. IT WILL NOT HAPPEN. Until the Managers take responsibility of their units and staff. The Lt. should've communicated with me, before they issued an action plan, when they knew I was working on written warning. They totally undermined me and what I was trying to accomplish. The Lt. stated they would do their own paperwork. I informed them that's fine, I don't have a problem with that. We also discussed with Capt, Lt, Unit /asst Managers should have a meeting amongst us, so we could all at least try and get on the same accord, but of course this never happen. On one occasion I had received a call from administration stating that the Warden would be ready to go downtown and the time. I talked with my supervisor, to inform them. I was going to ask one of the Lts. In EHU to cover until I returned. I called the Lt. and informed them I need someone to cover for me, they stated hold on and switched me to the other Lt. who agreed to come down and relieve me. Always some DAMN drama.

News & Observer file photos

Affairs, debt and murder

The crime: In July 2008, the victim was reported missing by a friend, nearly 8 hours after victim's husband said she went out for a jog and didn't return. Two days later, her body was found in an undeveloped area near the family's neighborhood. She had been strangled to death. As police investigated her death, a picture of a troubled marriage emerged. The defendant described victim, a stay-at-home mother, as a shopaholic who strained the family's budget. Her friends said defendant, an engineer, was neglectful, unfaithful and controlling. The defendant admitted to an affair with one of victim's best friends and said the couple, deeply in debt, had recently decided to separate. Police found unexplained scratches on the defendant's neck and said he cleaned the house and the trunk of his BMW the morning his wife went missing.

The outcome: The defendant was arrested in October 2008 and charged with first-degree murder, and temporary (later permanent) custody of his daughters went to victim's family. At the defendant's trial in April 2011, a detective testified that investigators found on the defendant's laptop zoomed-in satellite images of the wooded dirt road where victim's body was found. The investigators said the images were timestamped before the victim went missing. The defendant's attorney claimed the police planted that evidence and later called the judge "biased." The jury delivered a guilty verdict on May 5, 2011.

The case received international attention and was featured on NBC's "Dateline." The defendant's attorneys appealed the verdict and he was granted a new trial in early 2014. But before the trial could happen, he took a plea deal and admitted to killing his wife. He was sentenced to at least 12 years in prison but had already served five years at that time. According to the N.C. Department of Corrections, the defendant has a projected release date of Nov. 23, 2020.

The Sgt reported that two inmates were in a fight on 2nd shift and they were all scratched up. The Sgt was requesting to lock up 4 inmates. I talked with the OIC, in which we both agreed, that the inmates were not going to lock up. One inmate had a deep scratch to their face but would not tell what happen. I talked to the other inmate and they stated they did not know what happen, they must have scratched themselves in their sleep. Another inmate stated they were in the shower, when they looked out to see what was going on, the two inmates were or had been fighting. I handcuffed another inmate, when she started spilling the beans, the two inmates in question had been fighting. I was talking with another inmate and they stated "I don't talk to the Sgt or the assist manager. You are the only one I talk to. The inmate stated one inmate came around the corner and bumped the other inmate and it was on. They fought, and it was a good fight. When the police walked in, everybody went their separate ways. It was a good fight and a fight that should've happen a while ago. After they finished fighting, they were sitting there talking, laughing and crying. They were fine after they fought. I called the OIC and let them know I was going to lock them up. The OIC says to me, "well sounds like you are letting the inmates run that unit." "I stated no! so you are telling me if the inmates fight now, we don't lock them up?" The OIC stated "no this happens last night on 2ⁿᵈ shift, they have been this long, and nothing has happen." I determined that something did occur. I want them locked up!" The OIC stated "well I support you, but I need something in writing, as to why your staff didn't do what they were supposed to." "I will talk to the staff when they arrive for duty.

3/11/15 I called the gatehouse Sgt to inquire about whether or not security supervisors had returned from the outside hospital. The Sgt stated "yes." I asked, "where was the staff?" they stated, when they arrived back at the institution, they were instructed to report to the OIC, they assumed they had because; they remained at the armory checking in weapons. They turned in their weapons and the Sgt thought they reported. I called the staff on the other side of gatehouse. I ask them, if they had seen the staff and they said "no, they had not been inside the gatehouse." I ask them to check the gate log and they were still signed in. I called via radio to all areas; if the staff was in your area have them to call the OIC. I also made an overhead page several times, with no response. I called the Sgt to confirm what was passed on, in reference to staff assigned to those special areas. Staff was to work shift, until the normal schedule time to leave the facility and the Sgt stated "that is correct." I informed them about the staff returning to the facility and not reporting to the OIC as directed, by the Sgt. They exited the institution without authorization.

News Paperclip

A Guilford county woman was convicted of first-degree murder, conspiracy to commit murder and solicitation to commit murder November 23, 1993. The defendant's husband was stabbed to death in his home on March 13,1992. The defendant got two friends to kill her husband, promising to share the life insurance money with them. The defendant's parole release date is set for Aug. 1, 2022.

We received recertification training once a year with firearms, self-defense techniques, pepper spray, **UNDUE FAMILIARITY** which was one of our biggest problems. You have to be mentally strong having to deal with women and men. Men at a women's facility verses women at a male facility. If you know you don't possess this kind of strength mentally, do not set yourself up for failure or get fired!!! During my career there was never a time being undue with an inmate ever entered my mind. Sure, there were things said to me, but I did not engage. I dealt with it appropriately and kept it moving. Once you allow them to get in, they will always be there. There are attractive men and women smart, talented, college graduates that are incarcerated. Think about the last word you just read INCARCERATED!! You can be prosecuted people! Back in the day... old school it was not as prominent as it is now. Yeah, yeah! I know you're like this ain't old school, it aint dumb school either, this new school. MILLENIALS!!! Don't go to sleep on old school.

Herald Sun News Paper

September 1975 three defendants two male and female approached and rob a bank and fled. They ran through a stop light and was pulled over by the State Highway patrol. As the patrolman walk to the stopped vehicle, two of the defendants laid down in the seat. One of the defendants aim a sawed off shot gun out the back window and shot the SHP in the neck area, who later died. The defendants fled the scene. All available Officers were called to a soybean field to search for the suspects. A state helicopter arrived and landed to bring equipment. Upon the helicopter taking off the wind from the blades, opened the waist high soybean field. One suspect was spotted lying down between the two rows in the soybean field. The suspects were ordered to surrender. A second order was given to surrender, when the suspects stood up and did not give any resistance. The female was sentenced to 80 years in prison.

YEAR 1999

This defendant was charged in indictments with the first-degree murder of the victim, and possession of a firearm by a convicted felon. The jury returned guilty verdicts on both charges, with special verdicts finding first-degree murder by premeditation and deliberation and by lying in wait. Following a capital sentencing hearing, the jury returned a verdict recommending life in prison without parole. The court sentenced defendant accordingly and imposed a concurrent sentence of twenty-one to twenty-six months for the firearm charge. The evidence tended to show that the relationship between defendant and the victim, had been volatile for several years. In October 1999, the victim was trying to end the relationship, and began seeing two other women. Defendant responded by constantly paging and watching and harassing each other. Defendant had also explicitly threatened the victim, both directly and in comments the victim's brother. The victim told his friend that the defendant had told him that if she caught him with a new girlfriend, she would kill them both, but the victim believed she was just bluffing.

On Wednesday, 6 October 1999, defendant sent flowers to the victim at work with a card asking for "one more chance."

The following day defendant visited the victim at work and was seen sitting at a desk and talking with him.

The medical examiner testified that the victim suffered two bullet wounds, one of which entered his chin from an indeterminate distance. The other bullet had entered the front of his chest from only a few inches away, and the exit wound indicated that, at the time he was shot, the victim's back was pressed up against something firm, like the floor. The victim had also suffered a head laceration, which could have been caused by a fall down the stairs or by a blow from the butt of a gun. The victim's jacket had been pulled up behind his back and his pockets had been turned inside out and emptied. The cords to the victim's phone and caller ID box in the bedroom were cut.

We had our intake area that was responsible for transporting inmates out to various appointments. If an inmate missed their court date a bench warrant would be issued not for the inmate, but for the Warden, because it was their responsibility to make sure that inmate appeared on the date and time that was scheduled. There were almost always more appointments than there were staff to transport. We had to pull blood out that turnip, provide staff that we already didn't have to assist with transporting these inmates to various court and medical appointments. There were so many inmates that were transport out to the hospital. Then you being at an area hospital with inmates, some medical staff, give you push back, because the inmates are restrained, they feel they shouldn't be. They be trying to give them special treatment

No No No!! people this cannot happen. You should stay in your lane. You put staff, public and yourselves at risk when this happens. What they fail to realize is that, this inmate has been sentenced by a court and judged by jury, for a crime committed. Our main goal here is Safety and Security of the inmate, while they are away from the confines of the institution. This inmate could have just committed an assault on someone at the facility; so many things can happen in a split second. Then you have some that want to know what their crime was, which was irrelevant, to the healthcare of this inmate. Yes, they are inmates, but they are humans as we are and should be treated as such. There has been so many times that I have transported inmates out and the way the inmate was treated was terrible, to the point where I would have to say something to medical, of course which should always be reported. There were times that I had to take my Mom to the hospital, I would still have my uniform on. I noticed how they were treating her, they thought she was an inmate. OH no buddy I had to get them straight and let them know this was my Mother. What was going on with them, that they were not treating her appropriately. That day forwarded if I had to go anywhere or do anything with my Mom, I would take the time to go home and change out that uniform. I had to give accolades to the supervisor and their staff in that area mastering transports. The supervisor and the staff handled their business. If you are a supervisor staff don't mind working for because you handle yourself and your area, things will run like clockwork. Staff will make sure the job or task was completed. Staff would come in EARLY in the morning transport inmates, return and transport again. Staff would return from transporting and assist the shift on the yard dining hall or escorts, due to staff shortages. When you have people come together in any area and work diligently things will get done. I always tried to treat people the way that I wanted to be treated. I had staff coming to me volunteering to work off days weekends week days, because they knew shift was short. I could call them a home, or they would let me know ahead of time, they will work due to staff shortage. Then you have those that will pull against the grain and try to throw salt. We have had staff transporting in bad weather, this should never occur if we can help it. We jeopardize so much when this happen. It can be costly in the long run. No lives can ever be replaced. We would discharge inmates and the would be transported to the bus station, to travel home. If the inmate misses this bus, it didn't matter if they live on the Virginia line or Tennessee or Timbuctoo, someone had to take a road trip, provided there was no other transportation. Inmates that were released did not have a home plan and were released to a shelter. Upon new admissions coming in, you would have to check the screens to see if the inmate had ever been on a control screen for Intensive Con, Maximum Con, if so they would have to go back on that control, until a committee could decide whether to remove them from that status or leave them. We did have some very assaultive inmates.

News and Record

November 2000

The victim was doing nothing more than walking down the street when he was robbed of $10 and fatally shot, police and court records say.

Police charged three people Wednesday in the death of 18-year-old, It doesn't appear the victim in this case was doing anything wrong,' said police Sgt., who oversees homicide and other investigations. ``He was just a target.'

Investigators believe robbery was the motive but said the investigation is continuing.

That's really all it was. They took money from him.

Two women and one man were charged Wednesday afternoon with first-degree murder and armed robbery in connection with the Tuesday night shooting. The shooting took place about 11:45 p.m. Tuesday as the victim walked down the Street near the intersection. When officers arrived, the 18-year-old victim was lying on the road.

A police department news release said he had been shot one time in the back. He died early Wednesday morning after being taken to the hospital for surgery.

This is the 18th murder that police have investigated this year.

The suspects are being held without bond in jail.

YEAR 2000

Police officers were called to the home of 24-year-old panther football player, in charlotte to investigate the report of a person having been shot. When the officers arrived at the residence, they found the victim dead. In the house at the time of the shooting were his 25-year-old wife, and their newborn daughter. Homicide investigators questioned along with neighbors and other family members. The investigation revealed that wife shot her husband during a domestic dispute. On the night of July 6, 2000, it was revealed that the victim was returning home from a panther away game at Tennessee and upon entry to the residence, the defendant opened fire with a shotgun and shot her husband twice with the fatal wound being to the head. On November 5, 2003, the defendant was sentenced to nearly 8 years in prison due to her guilty plea to the charge of manslaughter recorded by the court august 2003. It was ruled that the slaying was premeditated and deliberate, and that she acted with malice, due to shooting her husband a second time after she rendered him helpless with the first shot. The defendant had purchased the plane ticket for the victim flying from Nashville to charlotte on the night of the murder and arranged for her brother to pick the victim up at the airport.

neither her mother, who had been staying with them or her five yr old son were at the residence the night of the incident. Police indicated that his keys were still in the front door and his luggage was in the foyer and the 12-gauge shotgun was on the floor.

YEAR 2006

The crime: On Nov. 3, 2006, the body of 29-year-old victim was found by her sister, strangled and bludgeoned in the home the victim shared with her husband, and their toddler daughter. The victim, pregnant at the time, had been struck in the head more than 30 times. The toddler, at home at the time but uninjured in the attack, was left alone there and had tracked the blood of her murdered mother through the house. There were no signs of forced entry in the home. The defendant was away on a business trip, staying at a hotel in at the time of the murder. But when police asked for the defendant's help in the case, he refused to cooperate. Investigators eventually concluded that the software salesman, who they said had a history of domestic violence and extramarital affairs, disabled a security camera in a side entrance stairwell of the hotel, made the 169-mile trip back to to kill his wife, and drove back to the hotel.

The outcome: In early 2009, The victim's mother won a wrongful death lawsuit against the defendant, and the victim's sister was awarded custody of the toddler. The defendant was arrested in December of that year and charged with murder. He pleaded not guilty. His first trial, in 2011, ended in mistrial, with the jury deadlocked 8-4 in favor of acquittal. He was found guilty in a second trial in March 2012. He is serving a life sentence. A key witness for the prosecution was a convenience store clerk, who testified that she sold gas to the defendant at 5:30 a.m. on the morning of victim's murder. In August 2017, a Wake County judge denied request for a third trial. This case got a lot of national attention, even making the cover of People magazine in 2007.

There were days that the facility lights would go out, as it was nearing dusk. When you take over your post, you are suppose ensure you have all your equipment and make sure it is working properly. When the lights go out, everybody would need batteries and flashlights for the most part, but WHY? Some of the dorm were not on generators, so you would be in the pitch-black dark. Think about being in this situation in a dorm by yourself with no lights. When the problem was found it would be some hours later. The facility has been all night or a half of night without power. When this happen, it causes a domino effect in the facility. One time I think a snake crawl in the box and a squirrel and blew the transformer. Let me tell you there were no boring moments at women's prison. One day I was standing out by the fence and I kept looking at it and looking at it. I walked closer to it, and it look as if there was damage being done to the fence. I reported it and other staff looked at it we looked at video, to see what was happening. LAWD and behold the squirrels were chewing on the fence causing this damage. I just could not believe it!!! NCCIW had a lot of squirrels chasing each other, mating running up and down the fences, setting of the alarms those things are terrible with those sharp teeth and claws.

8/15/14 @ 1620 The Sgt checked out a state vehicle and while driving the vehicle they were stopping at a traffic light and some equipment (Gun Holster) slid from under the driver seat. Upon returning to the facility the equipment was turned in and returned to the armory.

1936 The Officer returned from outside hospital and failed to turn in their equipment (gun Holster) that was issued. The Lt. was notified of the incident and upon the Lt. talking with the Officer they stated they did check out 2 holsters one right and one left. The Officer stated they were waiting to arrive at the hospital before putting on the other holster, because it was uncomfortable driving with both holsters on. Officer realized at 0643 that they had left the holster in the vehicle, failing to report they were missing equipment, because they thought the Officer returning would turn in the equipment. The Officer checked the vehicle in which she did not locate the equipment. The Sgt contacted the relieving Officer at the hospital, to check the room and contact security at the hospital. The holster was not located. However, it was found the day before and it was not reported up the chain. The search for this equipment could possibly been prevented, when the holster was found previously.

10/3/16 @ 1745 Lt. was walking from master control to the auditorium, when he found a can of pepper foam. The Lt. turned the pepper foam over to the Sgt to find out the owner. There was only one unit that used pepper foam, which was narrowed down quickly. The Sgt of that compared the serial numbers to the list of numbers that were issued by her and that number was not documented. The item was secured, and the other shift supervisors were notified. On 10/3/16 Officer arrive at the gatehouse to be checked in. after being checked in they placed their pepper foam in their coat pocket. 10/4/16 The Officer noticed a day later they did not have their pepper foam. It was reported to the unit Sgt by the Officer that the spray must have fell out her pocket on Friday. 10/5/16 the sgt informed the Lt. and the pepper foam was returned to the Officer.

Breast Cancer walk October held for the offenders and the staff family members or themselves, who suffered or passed from the disease would participate in this big event. This was another annual event, the offenders looked forward to. There was a vendor that would provide bagels in a breast cancer symbol. The units would come to the auditorium a unit at a time and make out their name tags and who they were walking for. The facility is very large, so it was roped off, where the inmates would walk and how many laps and the next unit would come and follow through, this would continue until all the units were allowed to complete the walk.

Kairos this event took place twice a year the offenders looked forward to this event also. This group brought in approved food items. The one thing everyone looked forward to was getting those cookies, staff and inmates.

RAMADAN inmates would have to be escorted to the dining hall first thing in the morning to receive their breakfast meal. You had those true Muslims and then there were those inmates that, used Ramadan and the Muslim religion as a crutch, to get their way or what they wanted like their head wraps, prayer rugs and the Karan.

RED BOXES Christmas time there were those red boxes, they would be brought in on a van loaded down and the inmates would be waiting to receive. These boxes had a lot of items in them of which had to be put on inmate's inventory with their personal property. Lordt every time something was confiscated, the inmate's first response was, it came in my re box. We always tried to keep a sample box, so we would have an idea of what was in it and what was not. Christmas time there would be several church groups arriving with food items to serve the inmates for Christmas. These inmates would eat sooooo much until it literally made them sick. The was a meal I guarantee no child was left behind. LOL

FOOD BOXES use to be received only at Christmas only, but now they receive them through the year. There would be so many, it would take 2 to 3 days to distribute them out. There again more staff needed, that would have to be pulled from the shift to assist. When you get it you better guard it with your life, because the ones that didn't have one would take your stuff if the opportunity presented itself. The pregnant inmate also had their little gathering through the social workers.

JULY 4th we also conducted events that consisted of competitions bag race, egg race, tug of war, the inmates would compete as units. The inmates enjoyed the games and it was something to occupy their time because they were all off from their assigned duties, except for the dining hall workers. When you gave them something to do, it kept down a lot of disruption. My mother would always say an idle mind is the devil's workshop.

NATIVE AMERICANS these inmates have figured out a way to get their nicotine fix on. When this came into play, these inmates would have a designated area where they went to smoke out of a pipe in a circle. At first the group was very small, then it began to get bigger and bigger. This was how a lot of inmates continued to smoke. A lot of the inmates abuse this privilege. Inmates would give other inmates their pipes and let them go smoke. Inmates would show up without a pipe and claim to be Native American. Later, it was found that the only way you were to participate in the group, only if you had received a pipe through the mail room. So, if you had not received a pipe through the mail, you would not be enjoying the luxury of Native American. This stop a lot of the inmates non-Native Americans from coming. The circle returned to its normal small size. Then the inmates began stealing, whatever that was that they were smoking. While they were in the circle and the Chaplain turned their backs just for a second, the hands was always quicker than the eyes. The inmates would get it and return it their building and split it amongst themselves. These items were stored in the Capts office. It's always had a very high aroma. The inmates would be out on the grounds trying to hide the rolled-up cigarette, but they could not hide the smoke coming out of their nose and mouth. LOL

LEADERSHIP TOUR Leaders from around different areas of the state, would come visit and tour the facility. They always seemed amazed at the daily activities that went on. They had many questions afterwards. There would be inmates assigned to speak to them and tell their story of how they became incarcerated.

DOG PROGRAM Also there was the dog program which was good for the inmates. The inmates would care for these animals 24 hour a day 7 day a week. The dogs would graduate from the program and then a new set of dogs would be brought in. Those dogs got more affection and protection from those inmates, than a human would. Of course, there was always somebody that was going to try and mess up everything. These inmates would be removed from the program. It has always been said the Dog is (wo) man's best friend

You have the semi-private dorms, housing 2 inmates to a room, mostly for the long-term inmates. One dorm housing reception/ new admission inmates and pregnant inmates. There were 5 buildings in this unit. Reception was to be manned with 4 staff at all times, which rarely occurred due to shortage of staff. Believe or not each shift was different. There were your dorm janitors that were assigned to clean mostly the common areas hallways, bathrooms, dayroom area during the morning hours. Inmates house inn the semi-private rooms were responsible for cleaning their own areas. Reception followed the same clean up schedule as the other quad dormitories. Then you have those inmates that don't want to work or help, causing problems just being in the way, of the inmates that were cleaning. All beds were to be made up military style. Staff would also monitor inmates preparing the cleaning solutions. Inmates would not like the janitor job, so what they would do they would go down to the quad and pour the cleaning products down the drain and say they were done cleaning. Wellllll you know, we know about how long it takes to clean a quad. Da! Then they would receive disciplinary and be removed from the work assignment. Inmates will do any and everything they could to get out of working, by getting medical documentation or bedrest. Inmates worst nightmare was the showers, had to be detailed meaning they would clean the tile with a toothbrush, to get in the crack and crevices. They were inmates that would clean, because they knew they had to get in that shower, and they wanted it to be clean. The staff were supposed to check behind them to make sure everything was clean, so the quad could be cleared for activities, ironing, telephone, television, blow dryers, hot irons and the canteen. Inmates linen was taken up once a week, clean linen issued. There were always those inmates that was the hoarders, try to have more than was then were supposed to. They would have extra pillows, sheets pillowcases, extra mattresses and covers. The stockroom was giving out more than they were getting back. Usually the inmates were appointed to give out and take up linen, so there you go. Then we would end up having to search inmates to recover all the extra items in their possession. In the special housing areas, inmates were putting their linen down the toilets stopping up the plumbing or utilizing them to mule items from one cell to another.

When a code was called in one of the special housing units. Back then we had glass coffee pots in certain areas. Well, staff responded, once I arrived staff was talking to this inmate, trying to get them to put down the broken piece of glass, that they were threatening to cut their neck with. Past experiences have always taught me, there is only so much talking you can do. Staff continued to talk and plead with the inmate, to put the broken piece of glass down. I decide it was time for this to end. While staff were keeping the inmate occupied, with their back turned to me at an angle, I made a move to secure the broken glass in their hand. Once that happen, other staff just kinda came in on top of me. I kept seeing blood on the floor. I checked the inmate they were fine. I ask the staff to check themselves, because someone was bleeding. The Capt stated to me, check yourself. When I held up my hand up to look, blood began to run down my arm, it was me! My finger was slashed somehow another. Once the inmate was secure, the Capt made me go get checked. Medical want to send me out to get stitches. I stated I was not go to ER for this little cut, give me some of those little stitch band aids and wrap it with a big band aid, I was fine and went back to my duties. There was another incident that occurred when staff was securing an inmate, the inmate was so aggressive that one of the staff started to falling head first to the floor. As I was assisting with securing the inmate, I observed the staff falling. I stuck out my hand and palmed, as the staffs face fell in my hand, I then push them backwards to get their balance. It scared me to death.

Once there was an inmate that swallowed 5 razors and had to be transported out to the hospital. The end result was no good. Inmates can just do some really crazy acts, like drinking each other's blood, like they might be vampires or something. There was always a trend of some sort, I think at this particular time it was the Gothic thing the black attire, fingernails, lipstick earrings and the hair. When you talk to them of course they would deny it. You would know if you see them because they would have little small cuts on them, just enough to be able to suck the blood. The one gross thing they would do, was drink menstrual, period, cycle blood, which ever one you want to call it.

There was med clinic list put out daily for inmates with the times they were to report for their appointment. Inmates would submit a request to be seen by medical for whatever ailments they were having. These inmates know they had appointments, especially the ones that were not assigned, to a work project. If they did not show, the staff would have to locate them, but why? Inmates would not show up to their work assignments and staff would have to locate them, but it was only so much they could do because they were in the dormitory by themselves. Inmates were also to sign out of their building when they were not working, so when they were summoned for whatever reason, you would know where they were. Inmates as usual would take advantage of the opportunity, not report to their assigned work area and be on the grounds with their friend(s) all day risking lockup or write up. There would be inmates that come up to master control and be shooting basketball on the court. I'M like "give me that ball, Why, are you up here shooting ball at 8:00 in the morning. Your quad has not even been cleared by staff for cleanliness." They would either go to another building or swindle staff to give them a ball or go to the gym. Staff should always be conscious of what goes on around you at all times, not just in prison but also outside of prison.

There was a time when inmates were allowed to receive personal property (only at women's prison) through our mailroom, which was a lot of man hours. These inmates would walk around with name brand items on, matching Victoria secret out fits, jeans, shoes and jewelry. They were dressing better than you and I and we are working. LOL Inmates had only on locker, they had sooooo much property they would have in their possession. If the inmate went to lock up, transfer or court it was a bad day, especially if you had more than one. These items had to be inventoried, you would have to indicate the name, new or used some type of identity, It was terrible most of the time you were by yourself. It seemed like you would never finish. While you are inventorying, the other inmates doing what they want, because you are tied up inventorying property. Then all this property had to be placed in white property bags that were not big at all. You would end up with 15 or 20 bags of property, to put in the warehouse. The 15 or 20 bags would have to have their own spot. You get in the warehouse; you get in the warehouse it's hotter than ten folds and you have to rearrange stuff to get this property in there. Perishable items (food) had to be placed in another area, so it would not get destroyed by the critters. Inmates were issued the maroon (bonnie) coats, they looked like they had air in them. Inmates would use them to hide contraband inside. Staff search an inmate and the entire sleeve was packed with cigarettes. Inmates are very crafty when it comes to hiding contraband. An inmate was search and staff found money, that had been folded very small, in a plastic bag in a lotion bottle, with the lotion. If you did not take the time to search these inmates and know how to search them, you will not find these items. You would know when they was holding something, either they become talkative, nervous or squirming about trying to throw you off of what you are doing. Inmates would hide contraband sometimes in places that they knew staff would not look and sometimes it would be right there in plain view right under your nose, your on work station. It may be what look like a piece of torn paper remove it, there could be something under it, string pull it there may be something on the end of it, dirty, nasty or smelly. They would hide stuff in places you would not believe. They will cut a small pocket inside their pants, just to hide contraband. If it looks suspicious, 9 times out of 10 you would find contraband, follow your instinct. You should be very thorough when searching an inmate. When you think back, you would be like there is a lot of traffic back and forth in a particular area. (RED FLAG) They would even through contraband on top of the building to hide it. When maintenance staff come to the area, not having to deal with population, they didn't know any better, they would get the item down at the inmate's request and the inmate lying to how the item or objects got on the roof in the first place. If an inmate has something on them when a supervisor shakes them down, 9 times out of ten you are done for. Inmates destroyed so much state clothing, attempting to be seamstresses playing sports bars and thongs out of the t shirts and the underwear, cutting out jeans, putting chemicals on them to fade them. Hell, they would use chemicals in their hair, when you them later, you be like how her hair get blonde.

All the units had a identification board, that would have to be maintained daily as movements occurred. The semi-private dorms utilize books, that contained picture IDs of the inmates housed in that area and the beds the were sleeping in. So that if staff work those areas, they would be able to identify, who the inmate was if they need to be located and staff would know who to look for. When the inmate was moved their ID pic was to be removed and take to the dorm they were moving to, instead of having print another picture.

Evening shift, inmates are starting to return from their work projects. There were inmates that wore white dining room workers and cosmetology. These inmates were supposed to change out of their uniforms after work. Well of course you had those that did not want to follow the rules and want to stay out on the grounds, with their friends. Some would be tired and wanted to take a shower and lay down. Then you got those inmates, that have been in the dorm all day doing nothing, creating havoc, for staff and the other inmates being loud, disrespectful, of the inmates that have worked all day and just want to rest. All the dorms had, what they call silent TV, where they could listen to the television with their own personal radio / headphones. There were inmates that did not have this privilege, because they were indigent. (no Funds) In order for you to be classified as indigent, you could not have had a certain amount of money in your trust fund account, for 30 days, I think. Then there were some inmates that did not have the equipment to watch TV or could not watch the channels they wanted, they would take the power cord to the TV, so that way nobody got to watch TV. In the afternoon the grounds would be crawling with the inmate population, sometimes there would only be 1 or 2 staff on the grounds., which there should be a staff from each unit. The amount of inmates out on the grounds during this time, anything was subject to happen. There was a volleyball and a basketball court the inmates could utilize. They would stay occupied for a little while until we had to break up arguments and fights. The auditorium had set times for the units to come up and utilize the gym area. As my Mom (RIH) would say " a idle mind it the devils workshop." Summertime sunbathing!! A policy was put in place each year. You know the (Caucasian) inmates has to have their tan, the Afro Americans were looking for that card table under the shade tree, air conditioner or a big fan. LOL You could walk out on the grounds and you would think you was at the beach, at least they thought they were at the beach. The next day you see inmates they were sun burned and hurting. They would have to go to medical, some would redder than a barrel of apples, skin peeling it was terrible. Inmate would have designated areas where they sunbath and the time. In one unit the inmates were allowed to have a cover on the ground, but one inmate to each cover. Sometimes there would be staff on the grounds and sometimes not. Inmates be having sex, we be watch in them on the camera. We knew what they would be doing. They would have the cover covering, but you could tell the motion. Staff would intervene and the inmates would be written up. Inmates hollering bloody murder all the way, "it wants me you saw," well the camera don't lie." That kinda shuts them down. LOL Inmates walking around with T shirts that they had to have a medical slip for, t shirts hanging out. This aint gonna happen on my watch. Then it seem like all of them were wearing t shirts. Then we had to pull them over and check to see if they had a slip. I would be on the grounds and then here come one with their pants down around their hips. WHY? "Pull yo pants up! Better yet go to your dorm and change out of those pants and bring them back to me. The inmates would get extra clothing or large clothing out of the laundry room basket in the unit, when someone was released. Inmates with their collars tucked in, shirt sleeves, shorts rolled up, "get right" this was a constant thing, but after a while I didn't have to say it, because it became automatic when the inmates saw me. I could see them from a distance pulling collars out, buttoning the shirts and pulling those sleeves down. There have been clothing change since I retired. I don't think the even have the collar shirts anymore.

We would be so glad when daylight saving time came in the spring, because it would give the inmates extra time out on the grounds, before it closed. The staff would be glad to. When they come in mostly everyone was trying to get a shower, watch a little TV and go to bed. Then you got your night owls and eagle owls trying to see and hear everything going on or a watch out person. When you hear "man down" you knew what was up. Inmates would quad hop. They would be in quads they are not assigned to and sleep in there all night, with their girlfriends. HOW? Then you have yo inmates that like to follow the crowd, trying to fit in somewhere or need the feeling of belonging somewhere. The inmates are young coming in and actually look at prison as a high school or college campus (Millenials)Then there was the **X** generation. The younger population that had to go to school, of course you had those that did not want to attend, because they thought they were grown and didn't have to. You would have to hunt them down on the grounds and escort them to their classes. They would make trouble in the classroom with the teachers, so they would get put out. I would make them go right back and dare them to cause problems again. They knew everything, you couldn't tell them nothing, they had all the answers. Asking "why I have to go to school?" Why not?" You would try and talk to them and tell them you need to finish your education. Utilize the tools you have while you are here. When you are released and return to society, you have to be able to do something else besides, be in the street drugging, barefooted and pregnant. When you go apply for a job, you can't answer the question about whether you have a GED, diploma or did you graduate, that's going to be the first strike against you. The next strike is you have been incarcerated felony or misdemeanor. It's already going to be hard to survive, so you try to use the tools you have here now, to help you transition back into society. If 2 out of every 10 I talk to listen and follow suit, it would be a wonderful thing. Then those other eight, who want to do their own thing, hanging on the grounds with their crew, getting in trouble and going to lock up. Inmates walking around with one pant leg up and one down. I guess trying to flag someone in a gang.. Inmates would stand on the rails in front of reception dorm H (new admissions) and talk or pick out inmates, they were going to be with when they were released off reception, throwing, passing, letters, notes and messages. Inmates on the grounds about to fight, you intervene, pull them into your office, sit them down and try to find out what the problem is. This is in between all the other duties you got going on. Most of the time inmate arguments come from he said, she said. Then they wanna try and argue in front of me. So I'm like "you hook on phonic and stuck on stupid, this is what other inmates want to see, entertainment, so they can have something to talk about tonight, when they are sitting with their friends eating oodles of noodles, Ho Ho cakes, watching Television talking about, who beat who ass and both are you are sitting in lock up scratched up, loss of hair and bruised up, is it worth it. I can't even count the many times that I have had this conversation. I would tell them "go down that hill running yo mouth and can't defend yourself. You gonna be fighting for a minute, before I get there. I ain't as young as I use to be, running to all y'alls fights breaking them up, before you get yo wig split open."

Usually you would know when something was about to go down, because you could see the crowds forming on the grounds (red Flag) or you would see little groups of inmates. Usually when I observed this, I would go out on the grounds and just show my presence with the Sgts and most of the time this would deter whatever was getting ready to go down. This would put the inmates focus on us, instead of whatever it was they were planning on engaging in. I had a great bunch of staff; they just couldn't count. LOL The Sgt handled themselves in a respectful manner and believe me, if we didn't everyone would know before the next day. I would just go sit down at a picnic (card) table, especially if I felt like something was going on. The inmates would then begin to leave one by one, until I was pretty much sitting there by myself. Inmate would walk up and say, "Capt.

Why you mess them girls up like that?" I be like" what you talking about, I just came to sit down." After a while I couldn't mingle with the population like I use to, I was bogged down with administrative duties, paperwork. Then I had to set a timetable to do things on certain days, to complete what you need to do. I was a BIG procrastinator: I own it well, because I was doing other things I loved to do. Inmates use to write grievances on staff, peers, housing, administration, to downtown. This was another way I got to communicate with the inmates, when I was stuck in paperwork for a couple of days. Inmates most of the time just need someone to talk to or someone to listen. I would have some responses that would come back from staff, that would be ghetto Fab. Well of course I could not use their responses. I would get with the staff and let them know, they have to remain professional at all times. I would have a general response, that I would use and most of the inmates would agree. I had very few appealed grievances. The Sgt was the middleman, they had it all to do from the staff, administrative, inmates and the paperwork.

I had an inmate that entered my office stating, she needs to talk to me about something, adding I don't want this to go any further. I'm like well there is a reason for you telling me what happen (red Flag). The inmate continued to explain, that another inmate did this to her face. The inmate pulls her hair back from her face. I observed red marks on her face. I ask her "what happen?" They stated, that another inmate, which was her roommate, got mad because them and another inmate, went to eat without them and the inmate scratch them they think. HUH!

The inmate says "I don't want to do anything, but if you move her everything will be ok. Well they did get moved. I advised the inmate that things would be handled accordingly. As I was on the phone, both inmates went into the laundry room. I talked with the other inmate, they stated their roommate grabbed them around their throat, with both hands, which left marks on both sides of her neck. I advised both inmates they would be going to lock up pending an investigation. The reporting inmate became very upset, stating "that's why no one tell y'all anything. That's why I didn't tell you what happen before, I knew you would lock me up." I again inform the inmate it was for investigation and their safety. Inmate stated, "what if I refuse." I ask refuse what." I then stated to the inmate "don't cause a disruption because it would not be pretty."

The inmates had hobbies making craft items, that they crochet or drawing, very talented individuals and smart. Inmates would make the craft items a lot of times to go out through visitation. When the staff search them there would be contraband hidden inside. Craft items were also used to hide contraband in the room sitting on inmates' bed. Staff was like "oh that's nice or it's so cute" all the time the contraband they are looking for would be sitting right there looking at them. Inmates would hide items in the door opening where the door lock, tie a string o it and when search was over pull it out, in the vents, light fixtures, books on the book shelf, tape things to the back of the book shelf, in the table leg, under the table, they had so many hiding places.

There would be times severe thunderstorms would come through the area. If you hear thunder you can bet yo bottom dollar, it's lighting. The grounds would be closed, and do you know so of these crazy inmates, would stay on the grounds. Then we risk getting struck by lightning, trying to run them inside. They would stand out in the rain and get soaking wet. The was always a yearly tornado drill, this was statewide, unfortunately it would always happen on a clear day. Staff and inmates are directed to what the procedure are inside and outside their buildings for safety. I wanted it to be done when a thunderstorm was coming up, so the inmates would think it was real. I am scared to death of a thunderstorm, mostly lighting, however, this is when people want to call and talk to you on the telephone. Lighting travels through the telephone and will make it ring people. Well I ain't answering, I don't care who it is. I was always taught when the LORD is doing his work, you need to sit down and be quiet until the storm is over. I have witness the damage lighting can do. My Mom and Aunt's house was struck by lightning. Then you had what you called lighting rods on houses, our house had a chicken sign with North, South, West, East on top of the house. The lighting knocked the chicken off the house, traveled to the attic knocked out the light and socket, knocked out the double plate light switch in the kitchen, my mom's car was in the drive way, it knocked the railroad tie out the ground onto my mom's car, destroying the electrical in her car, went through the ground hit a tree and you could see where it traveled up the tree and came out. So noooo I don't play with that Friends.

I was on the corner smoking a cigarette and I heard these sirens. I said to myself they sound like they are chasing someone. I was walking headed back inside, when the chase proceeded pass the prison. The car that was being chased didn't even stop at coleman and MLK someone could have been killed. Then I heard a big crash, I was like Oh my God, they have ran into someone. Well you know, when you talk to the inmate population, that's how you get informed I was talking to this inmate, who is in the revolving door, repeat offender. I ask them why they couldn't stay out of prison and they began to tell me what happen, the reason they returned. They started telling me about how they ran from the police, police were chasing them. I kept listening to them and I said, "that was you!" They said "yep, it was me, but they would have never caught me, if I hadn't dropped my wallet, when I jumped over the fence," she fell out laughing. I told her she could have killed someone.

I was leaving work along with some other staff. When I got to the stop sign, I notice this car, sitting in the middle of the road, with someone sitting inside. I jump out my car, along with a couple of other staff. We approached the vehicle, the person inside was unconscious. The doors were locked, so there was no way to enter the vehicle, so we called 911. The first responders arrived and began to bang on the window, this person finally started coming around. It appeared they had a diabetic episode. It was scary because we did not know if this person was dead or not.

When I was on the PERT team, I would get a call overnight stated, PERT was activated 02:00 in the morning. The adrenaline rush you would get, was awesome. I had all my team members set up on group text (technology) all I had to do was touch a button and the message was sent out to everybody, about the activation. They already knew the protocol. We would be given a destination to meet as a Battalion. When we arrive at our destination, it was huge 200 + PERT members. You could see the expression on the staff faces, as WOW! Y'all are deep, but we were also the elite!! Steam roll right over you. Moving quickly in formation, being about business.

One night we were activated, upon us arriving and getting our assignments, we were dispatched out to different areas, due to an escape. Myself along with 2 other members, were sent to Durham. We went down this little street, it felt like we were closed in. I was closed in, because I was in the back seat of the security vehicle, with a cage locked in with no way out, unless the door was opened from the outside. So, as we started down the street, I told the driver, this don't feel right, we need to get the hell out of here! Now! There was only one way out and that was the way we came in. They them attempted to turn around, which was impossible. I told them they need to back this thang up and get us the hell out of here. We found out later that this was an area that was known for illegal activities. So, then we go to the Hotel, because we received a report that the inmate had been sited. There was a lot of moving and shaking going on. We finally were called back to command, we were on I-40. I was still sitting in the back behind the cage, I felt the car swerve. I told the driver to pull the damn car over!! Because they were sleep, of course they denied it. I told them again to pull the damn car over! I couldn't do anything; I am locked in here behind this damn cage. Lawd help me it we get in an accident. I wouldn't be able to get out. So, they pulled over, I drove back to command safely.

There were several mock escape drills conducted to prepare us for the real thing. Teams were split up and sent different ways. I remained at command which was the PERT bus. The teams had been out for a while, but I could hear the dogs barking at a distant. The barking sounds as if it was getting closer and closer. I was listening to the radio traffic, as I walk off the bus to listen better to the barking, I heard someone moving under the bus. I YELLED!! They under the bus! They under the bus! Immediately command was locked down and sealed up. I was locked out the bus unfortunately. I ran and positioned myself behind a vehicle, to gather myself, my adrenaline pumping. We had no idea they would back track to the command post. I waited as other members trickled back slowly. One of the escapees decided, they was going to take one of the vans, that still had the keys in the ignition. I'm thinking to myself, if they take that damn van, we will never find him. So, I creeped up to the van as they was trying to start it. I grabbed them with one hand and threw them out the van, pure adrenaline. This little individual was so angry with me, because I threw them out the van like that. I ask them, was they ok? Did they get hurt. They would not say anything to me, they were embarrassed, I think. The others were picking at them, because they were a part of some special forces team and I threw them out that van like they were a piece of paper. They laughed and joked about it for the longest. I told them don't underestimate womens prison.

Two-night training exercise, we had a few members that were new to PERT and this was their first experience being out in the field, so they were excited. The newest members would be learning how to, utilize a compass to maneuver them through the woods to their destinations and return. Teams were split and sent different ways. Dark had set in for a while now, most of the teams had returned except for one, they were lost in the woods somewhere with the dog. There was a team sent back into the woods to find them. Later, you could hear the dog's faint bark, from no bark at all, so this was a plus. The dogs bark was getting louder so we knew they were on the right track, to return to command. Upon them arriving they were so exhausted as well as the dog.

6/18/11 @ 1100 I received a call for activation, upon arriving received information, we were deployed to Charlotte, inmate did not return from work release. Charlotte is a busy, busy place the feel of a little New York. We check hotels, truck stops, places that there were sitings of the inmate. 1740 we received information that the inmate was in custody in Union county. The inmate was returned to our custody and transported back to NCCIW for housing in segregation.

There was another inmate that was in Charlotte that had been released, but they had not completed their sentence. We proceeded to Charlotte to secure and transport inmate back to the facility. We met the probation officer, looked at the areas we needed to search. When we call the inmate, it was explained, what had happened, and we were there to transport them back to Raleigh. The inmate stated, "no they were supposed to be released." They were going to get in contact with their lawyer. The lawyer called, it was also explained to them and the inmate needed to turn themselves in. The lawyer checked out all the information given to them, stating they understood. They would talk to the inmate and try to convince them to turn themselves in. Well that of course did not go over well. After being in the area trying to locate this individual, dark fell upon us. The inmate called several times stating they were going to turn themselves in. We were staked out in front of their parent's home. The inmate requested that we leave, because our presence was upsetting their family and they would turn themselves in. They were told that was simply not going to happen. Later, that evening a car pulled in the driveway. The PPO pulled in the drive behind the car to block them, followed by us. The inmate got out the car attempting to talk to their family members as we allowed them to once they were secure. The inmate was placed in the security vehicle and transported back NCCIW.

12/1714 code two (count) was called, I ask the desk Officer who was we waiting on to call in their count, because the count was not clear, the Raleigh unit had not called in their count. I called the Sgt and ask, what was going on with the count. They stated they were going to conduct another count, which then they informed me they were missing one. I ask have they informed their manager. Meantime I had my Sgt to go down to the unit and conduct a count. While all this was going on, I received a call from the gatehouse stating 911 was on the phone. I'm like 911!! Why would they be calling me. 911 operator stated, there was a lady on the phone, saying she had been released by mistake and she was at the greyhound bus station, they wanted to turn themselves in. WHAT!!!! I spoke to the police officer, who gave me the name. It was our inmate. I immediately dispatch Sgt and staff to that location to take custody of this inmate. The inmate was transported back to the facility and house in segregation. **News paperclip**

June 2015 An Ex Correctional officer faced several charges after an inmate escaped from a male Correctional facility. The EX, correctional officer was charged with sex with and inmate, harboring a fugitive and aiding and abetting a fugitive. Her bond was set at $500.000. The Ex officer work as a food service officer.

A Ex Sergeant was arrested at a Correctional facility and charged with trying to bring drugs into a prison. Felony Conspiracy to deliver Marijuana and Suboxone

This is how most of the drugs come into these facilities (DIRTY STAFF) It's sad because this is what the public fall back on, when there is true staff during their jobs. This hurts us tremendously. There will be many more Dirty Staff, trying to make that quick money. As I had stated before most of the ones doing this, I feel like they already know the inmates before getting hired. Why? Because they don't try and hide the fact that they are Dirty.

PERSONAL SITUATIONS

I did eventually give up PERT because my Mom came to stay with me in 2010, I think and whenever I got a called out in the wee hours of the morning, my Mom would say, "you leaving, you gone be gone all night." I felt bad leaving her, so I gave up PERT. My Mom met a lot of my DOC family. They got to know and love her to. I would tell my coworkers how independent Mom was at 87 years old, she was still driving. My mom would take walks during the day when I was at work. This one guy would watch out for her for me. I would call her on the phone, the phone would ring and ring. I would call her back and she would answer. I would ask her "why you not answering the phone," she would tell me "I was on the phone." I would say to her "that why there is calling waiting on the phone," so she says to me, "well you just need to wait! until I finish talking. "I was to done. I got home from work one day, Mom and I was talking, and she started laughing, I ask her what she was laughing at, she stated to me" I walked up to the store today and I was crossing the street. I had my glasses in my coat pocket, they drop out and I didn't know it. When I turned around the glasses were laying in the road. "I ask her what did she do? She said, "I held my hand up to stop traffic (6 lanes Glenwood ave) I went and got my glasses out the road." I told her I know them drivers were saying look at this crazy old lady out here, they probably thought you were homeless. Mom says they might have, but I went back and got my glasses. I told my Mom I was going to get a call one day, that you been hit by a car.

One day I called my Mom and she told me she had been to food lion. I ask her how she got there, she told me "I walked (again crossing 6 lanes of traffic) but I want ever do that again. Those cars be flying out there on that road." So she got to the grocery store, brought groceries, knowing she could not carry all that stuff back, so she had someone in food lion to call her a cab. I ask her why she just couldn't stay at the house, until I get off work. I will take her where she needs to go. Mom say's I like getting out walking, exercising, going to the mailbox, just getting fresh air.

I called her one day she was at Walmart. Well mother how did you get there? She says I walked, she had brought some items, she said "I am waiting on the bus now to go back home." I told her she needed to stay right where she was, I was on my way from work to pick her up.

This particular day, I was about to get of work, I called Mom to see if she needed anything, before I got home. Soooo Mom says I went to Crabtree Mall. Well Mom how did you get there, she says "I rode the bus." I went into the shoe store, I brought me two pair of shoes. When I got ready to pay for them, I didn't have my little purse. I told the man, I would send my daughter by to pick them up, if they hold them for me. I told her yes, I will go by and pick them up. I got off work, went to the mall, to pick up the shoes. I told the cashier; my Mom was in here earlier and brought to pair of shoes. I was there to pick them up for her. The cashier says "yes, I remember her," he had the shoes at the checkout counter, ringing them up. The cashier asks me, "who was that lady that was with her, she was kinda weird." I had no idea what he was talking about. I got home and ask Mom was someone with her, she said "this lady was showing me how to catch the bus and she was following me." Oh Lord! "I told her somebody gone be done carried you off somewhere, nobody gone know a thing. The description my mom gave, it sounded like a homeless person.

I came home from work; Mom is usually sitting on the couch watching TV. I proceeded back to the bedroom, she was in the bed. I ask her "what was wrong," Mom says "nothing" I said "you sure" Mom says "I told you, it want nothing wrong." I turn around to walk away, Mom says "I fell" you fell. Where did you fall, what's hurting you? I knew you were lying in bed for a reason. Mom says "I was walking to the store; I tripped over the sidewalk and fell on my arm. I was doing everything I could not to fall. I didn't want to hit my head on the sidewalk. So, I fell on this arm." Well, she couldn't move the arm. I told her I would take her to the emergency room, she said "no I'll be ok. The next day I came home from work, I check her to see how the arm was. It scared me ½ to death when I looked at her arm. When I looked at the arm, she was black and blue on the left side down to her waist. I told her "get up get your clothes on, you are going to the ER NOW! We arrived at ER, Mom was sitting by the door, I was sitting across from her. I could see the Dr. on his way to the room. When he came through the door, he grabbed Mom's arm and raised it over her head, there was no pain. When she tried to raise it, she couldn't because it hurt soooo bad. The Dr stated she had torn her rotator cup, he put her in an arm sling, which made the arm feel a lot better, referred her to the orthopedic. When I went to work the next day, some of my coworkers said to me, they probably thought you were abusing the elderly. It was something to think about, because she was severely bruised. I would never ever do that to my mother or anyone for that matter. However, she did go to the orthopedic and they would not do surgery but put shots in her shoulder. I never heard her complain about the arm/shoulder again.

Throwback Officer Ford

1/10/90 new admission in from county jail with drug withdrawal. Inmate was escorted to medical. The inmate ask me, was there anything they could give her, for her drug withdrawal. I ask her when she talk to medical staff, did she ask them, she stated they said they would see. I told her I would try to find out once they get done with another inmate. Meanwhile, inmate was sitting in the lobby couldn't sit still, twisting, turning, slump over in the chair, very edgy. I ask medical if there was anything that could be given to the inmate for withdrawals. They stated that the inmate was going to be admitted to the infirmary.

1/19/90 Assigned to Single Cell, I heard a noise like a door opened. I checked it out and everything appeared to be secure. I heard the noise again, I went to investigate, the inmate was out of her cell, talking to another inmate. I then notified the Sgt. Who stated they would be right there. I told the inmate to "get back in that cell and close the door. The Sgt. Entered the building and proceeded down the hall, talking to the inmate, asking them how they they were getting out the cell. The Sgt. Moved the inmate to another cell, because they could use a comb to open the door, another inmate coached the Sgt. as to how to how the door was being opened. Once the other inmates figured it out or the inmate schooled them, how it was done then they all started coming out their cells. Then maintenance had to come and put a metal piece on the cell doors where the latch was, to prevent it.

1/20/90 Assigned to Single Cell relieved 2nd shift, they brief us that the other inmates were coming out of their cell. When I made rounds, the inmate stated to me. If they were not moved, they were still going to come out of their cell, that was the only way they would move them. This inmate was trying to get on the same hall with another inmate, that was move last night by the Sgt. Several inmates cursing back and forth at each other. One inmate asks another inmate for a cigarette, the inmate told them, they didn't have any. Then the inmate started to beat and knocking on something in their cell. I went to investigate, inmate stopped beating and banging when I approached their cell, she was sitting on the bed looking foolish. I ask them " why are you knocking." I might as well been talking to the damn wall. Once I left their immediate area, she started banging again, then a Big BOOM of thunder came over. The inmate stopped banging and went to sleep for a while. LOL

1/21/90 Single Cell absolutely off the chain. Relieved 2nd shift the officers and Sgt. in building searching inmate's property. The Officer informed me that, inmate was moved from one hall to another, because they were coming out the cell, walking the halls all day. The inmate was moved to the other hall, asking for cleaning supplies, to clean their cell. The Lt. Stated "no" not until in the morning. Then the inmate stated" you better call got damn Mental health, because I'm coming out this cell, it's nasty in here. The Sgt call and stated to me do not go down that hall by myself., only if there are two officers. Later, there was a key added to key count, for two padlocks for latches on the cell door.

1/25/1990 Single Cell relieved 2nd shift inmate was crying and mumbling "let me out of here," inmate requesting to go to Mental Health. The Sgt was notified. Then another inmate wanted to talk to me. Telling me everything that, led up to the day their children were killed, asking me if I saw them on TV, when they were carried to court. Sgt. in the building making a check, talking to the inmate requesting to go to mental health.

2/2/1990 Single Cell I was the floor Officer when the staff from 2nd shift stated, that this inmate was permitted to have cigarettes. I called to verify with my Lt, I was advised that the inmate was not allowed to have anything. The inmate asks me "why not?" I told them it was on their paperwork, that they were not allowed to have cigarettes or matches. The inmate told me, if they didn't get a cigarette, they were going to bust their head open on the wall. They stated she would spit in my face. I walked away. Later, upon me making rounds, the inmate stated they were throwing up blood, in the toilet, they told me to come in their cell. I ask the inmate "why?" but they didn't reply. When the Sgt came to make rounds, they talked to the inmate and they stated "touch me mother fucker, you won't touch me no more. "Then another inmate began to complain about a wrapping on their arm was to tight, their hand/wrist was still swelling from a fall. Lock up is off the chain right now. The inmate hollering, yelling about she want a cigarette, then began to throw shit out of her cell, water, urine, trash and kicking the door. I then secured their food trap door. The inmate continued to throw water. I notified the Sgt. and the water was turned off, all the inmates complaining about the noise. Then about 0500 another inmate starting to act up, being loud. Myself along with other staff, went down the hall to clean up all that shit, that the inmates had thrown in the hallway.

2/3/90 back in lock up, I was passed on from 2nd shift that it was a quiet day. I told them I guess so they (inmates) were up all night. This same inmate was awake stated, to me "she was sorry for the way they talked to me." The inmate then asks for 2 Tylenol and a cigarette. I told them they still could not have a cigarette. The inmate stated, "ok I understand. Then they ask for some panties. I gave them one pair of panties, as they stood at the door naked as a jail bird, not a boring minute.

2/11/90 Assigned to lock up (Wide Open) two inmates being escorted over, that were brought in from the half-way house. Inmate requested that their trap be opened, they wanted to see the Sgt. Inmate complaining about a headache, stating something popped in their head, they were going to die. Then another inmate told them, it was just the lights being turned out, they thought it was their head.

2/22/90 Lock up the same inmate requesting some fast teeth for their dentures. Why? You're going to bed. I called and talked with the Capt., who stated inmate was still not to have anything in their possession, due to their behavior. The Sgt. ask me how their behavior was. I stated it was alright, they were asking for a lot of stuff. Inmate still cannot smoke, they will have to wait until the next day, when the 2nd shift Capt. returns.

2/23/90 Relief Officer relieving staff for breaks, in the infirmary assisting staff with getting an inmate into bed. I went to Single Cell and relieved staff, the staff ask me to look at the door on the hall, where the inmate had literally kicked or knocked the door completely from the lock, just totally destroyed the cell door. Exited SC proceeded to the control center, inmate transported in on ambulance from the county, who had been having seizures in court. Notified the Lt. Lt. out to talk with the EMS staff, then medical. Inmate was sent out to the hospital with the deputy from the county.

3/23/90 I was sent out as a security supervisor. My Capt. stated in line up, if the inmate walks out the hospital, just don't even worrying about coming back to the unit. This was due to another incident happening a couple of days ago. Two staff transported inmate to ER 1 season staff, 1 new staff right out of basic training. The inmate went to the bathroom and walked right out on the other side and escaped. I told the Capt. I want carrying a weapon for nothing. I am not about to lose my job for no inmate.

4/3/90 assigned to Tower 1 Gatehouse now. The housekeeper entered who I knew. There was another man that walked up to the gate, before I opened the gate, I ask "how can I help you?" The other staff verified that they, was the new housekeeper working at the infirmary. Listening to other staff, I assume that this wasn't his first night coming in at 0300 which is never a good idea to do, at this time of the morning. I was made out an ass.

Trusting my fellow coworker. I let them enter into the facility, to that area. Then I received a call from the Lt. asking who they were. I told the Lt., the Lt. then stated to me, they didn't know anything about this person, being here this early in the morning. I got my ass snatched behind listening to another staff, trusting they knew what they were talking about. Lt stated, "we just can't let these people walk in here, when they get ready. I tried to explain that it was verified. The Lt stated they are to know about every moment going on at this compound. If I didn't know, I need to call and ask somebody.

5/17/90 Assigned at the infirmary staff escorts 4 new admissions and informs me, that 1 inmate has threaten the other inmate, that came in with them, about something that happened while they were in jail. I was also informed to be cautious with another inmate, that may be planning to escape. Notified my Sgt of the information I received.

6/1/90 Assigned to infirmary. Inmate had been asking, if they could smoke a cigarette, I told them they would have to wait. The inmate continued insisting on smoking. My reply was the same as 5 mins ago. While staff and I were busy trying to get the count straight with the staff on the phone, the inmate insisting on smoking got missing. The staff ask me had I seen them, I told staff no. Then we began looking for this inmate, all over the infirmary. We knew they were inside, because they could not get out, unless the door was opened from the inside. I ask the inmate's sitting in the lobby area, had they seen the inmate, they stated the inmate was in an inmate's room. I went in the inmate's

4 bed suite and ask, had they seen a tall white blonde inmate and they stated no. Still couldn't find this convict. An inmate came to the other staff and told them where the convict was. When the staff entered the room, the inmate stoop down behind the bed hiding. We let them know they were not even supposed to be back here in the inpatient area. Inmate was escorted back to the lobby and instructed to sit there and don't even think about moving unless they ask. I reported this to the Capt. who then informed the Sgt, to come over and have prayer meeting with this inmate.

6/5/90 Lock up Inmate requesting to get some more panties, because the ones they had had gotten to small. I informed the Capt. Who instructed me! To check, to see if the panties were to tight, if so, take those panties and give her another pair. I stated "I'm not looking at nobody else draws. I don't even look at my own draws. LOL Nobody can tell what size draws I wear just by looking at them. I'm not telling anybody; I need to see their draws. I told the inmate the Sgt was on their way; they could talk to them about that matter. Sgt in making rounds 2 inmates were talking about, what went down at another facility and they were not involved, BUT you are here in lock up. They felt like they were being set up, about the drug thing that went down. The ring leaders was back in population. The inmate they beat up, has been discharge from the facility.

6/6/90 lock up Inmates asking what are they suppose to do. They are being charge for something they were not involved in. The inmate's expressed to me, that they had submitted a grievance concerning this, when they were transported back here from the other facility. They were placed on the hall with the Death Row inmates, who was mad. Other inmates making threat to them. At the time there were only 2 inmates on Death Row. Later, on the Capt. called me and stated, for me to go ahead, take off tomorrow (Thursday). I stated to the Capt. "you still want me to work Friday night. Capt. ask me to work tomorrow night, Thursday night my scheduled day off. I stated "no" It's Friday. They stated they did not need me to work Friday, come in on Thursday though. I called and ask could I be off Thursday and work Friday. The Capt. stated we just barely have coverage, which this is all the time. Capt. was going to let me be off on Thursday night. It wasn't even my night off. When I ask for the night off, they always tell me they don't have coverage. Snake! LOL I'm just all damn confused now.

6/11/90 Security Supervisor I had returned with and inmate from outside medical. The Sgt ask me did I still have my equipment, I told them "yes." They stated I would be taking out an inmate to area hospital. While the Sgt was waiting for Officers to exit outside with the inmate, the Sgt get a call from the Capt. who stated, an inmate was in labor in the dorm. The Sgt went to pick up more equipment, thinking the inmate would be transported. The original inmate was escorted out of the unit about 2am. The Sgt retrieved some equipment, goes to the hospital and sit in the parking lot, for security reasons, due to some information they receive prior. I call and ask the Capt. was a security vehicle supposed to leave the facility with ½ or less than ½ of tank of fuel. The Capt. states, we couldn't send security vehicles out for security supervisor, because we need them. I stated to them, that I was told the car is not supposed to leave with a ½ or less than a ½ tank of gas. The Capt. stated that's during the day, a car should not be brought back without gas. It should be carried to the motor pool and refueled, before returning to the facility.

9/17/90 Assigned Infirmary -I had inquired with the Lt. about what I would have to do to take the Sgts examine, in November. They stated I would have to write a letter to the Capt. Telling them, I plan to make a career at NCCIW. If I wanted to move forwarded, by taking the Sgts examine. I would have to get a waiver. The Capt. Will get the letter to the appropriate people.

919/90 Assigned lock up – We had two inmates to Escapee. All of management attended line up and informed 3rd shift, once we relieved 2nd shift staff, they were to report to the lineup room. No one goes home at this point. The other lock up dorm had a busy night, moving safekeepers around to make room for regular population inmates, being brought over to segregation. Then we had an inmate that started acting a fool, throwing water, lotion out the cell. Inmate stating move them to Single Cell. They want to be by themselves. Earlier the inmate had sheets tied up around the bars, they were instructed, to take them down and they complied. I went back later; they had put those sheets back up. I took the sheets down and removed them from their cell. Sgt in the dorm to talk to inmate, who stated they wanted to go to Single Cell or give them some morphine, stating they could not take this. Then the inmate started clapping, singing. Officers entered escorting more inmates to be locked up. Then we heard the inmates screaming and yelling FIRE! She started a fire!! The Sgt and I immediately approached the area, while the inmate was standing in the cell. They had made a pile with sheets, paper and attempted to start a fire. We entered the cell, handcuffed and removed the inmate and the evidence, where ashes of the bed sheets had been burned. The inmate was escorted to Mental Health. 12:00 2 escapees had been captured, transported back to the facility and escorted to Single Cell; one was placed in the other lock up unit.

9/25/90 Single Cell – The Capt. Called me and ask me about the dates, that an inmate was admitted to SC, the only dates they had were in a logbook. My documentation had the Sgt/Officer escorted this inmate to SC 9/21/90 from Mental Health. The inmate left lock up unit 9/20/90 escorted to mental health by the Sgt.

9/25/90 Tower 1 – I received a response back from the Capt. Concerning the Sgts examine, which had my application and a note from the Capt. stating that "you are short 1 month, to take the Sgts examine. We encourage you to apply the next time."

9/30/90 Security Sup – When I called in my check, I informed the Sgt, that I had death in my family, I wanted to see if I could switch days off. Talked with the Capt. they stated it would be fine. The Officer that I was going to switch days with, would need to write a note, sign the note as an agreement between the both of us. I traveled to Boston Massachusetts for a funeral. We stopped in Philadelphia at my Uncle's house, who actually drove us to Boston. This was the longest drive; I had ever been on. It seems like we riding to the end of the Earth.

10/01/90 Single Cell – I was telling the Capt. And Lt. about the letter, I received from the day shift Capt. about the examine. Lt. stated "you are waiting for an answer from administration, so just disregard, that until you hear something from administration.

10/06/90 Tower 2 – After line up the Sgt approached me and began to congratulate me. I stated, "why are you congratulating me?" the Sgt stated "your name was submitted to PERT team. You need to meet with the day shift Capt."

10/9/60 Tower 2 – The Capt. Gave me note stating for me to send an application for the Sgts examine, to the individual name on the note by 10/10/90. I received a letter back from administration, requesting a wavier for me to take the examine. I had to fill out another application. Then I filled out the wrong application.

10/15/90 Unit Infirmary – The Sgt requested I go to the control center and assist another Sgt with new admissions. I was informed that the county was bringing a safekeeper. 1am county arrives with new admissions (SK) who was screaming, yelling being uncooperative, kicking, biting at staff and the deputies. This inmate continued with these shenanigans. Once they were placed in a safekeeping dress, inmate complied to have their ID made. We then escorted them to Mental Health. Once the inmate finishes processing, they were provided a paper gown. Once we exited their cell, the inmate went and jump feet first in the toilet, just standing there. I guess the water felt good to their feet.

10/19/90 Infirmary – During Line up the Lt. read a memo about me joining the PERT team, I relieved 2nd shift. The 3rd shift Sgt entered the infirmary talking shit. Had no idea what the problem was. 12:13 2 Sgts entered escorting an inmate by wheelchair, due to them having some type of seizure. Inmate was seen by medical and admitted. Inmate stated they were having chest pains their hands were numb. Once the inmate was checked and process, medical staff rolled them back to their bed, the inmate got up out the wheelchair by their self, went to the bathroom, came back to bed, laid down and went to sleep. WOW!

10/20/90 Infirmary – Relieved 2nd shift this one inmate was having their self a little party tonight, causing pure havoc in the inpatient area. They ask me was I there to pick them up. I ask them "pick you up for what?" they said, "to go to Single Cell." I told them "no." Oh lawd what I say that for, the inmate started shouting, for medical to bring them some water. Then they stated "this ain't no hospital, that's why I want out of here." Medical talked to her, the inmate calmed down for a while, then they said they were not feeling well. I ask them "what's wrong?" they said "my head hurts and I feel dizzy." I informed medical of their complaint. When medical went to talk to the inmate again, they said "I want my bed back, I can't sleep on this floor." Inmate's bed was removed due to them having seizures. The inmate said "I can't help I have seizures. Then the inmate went off, right on over to left field. The inmate finally calmed down and went to sleep.

10/22/90 Infirmary – Dealing with the same inmate. The inmate had thrown all that crap out of their cell, in the hallway. I informed 2nd shift, they need to get that stuff up before they leave. The Officers stated the inmate threaten to throw urine on them, if they try and clean up the mess. I called the Sgt and informed them. They said the same thing, Officers need to clean up mess before they leave. I went to the inmate door to see what was going on with them. The inmate was lying on their mattress and had appeared to have injured their hand somehow. I notified the supervisors, who came over, so the inmate could be checked by medical. The entire time 2nd was trying to get out of there. I told them they couldn't leave right now, because we may need their assistance. Lt. open the door, went in along with Sgts and myself, to see what the inmate had done. The inmate stated, "she was not concerned." Ok so why should anyone else be concerned. The inmate started talking shit to medical stating "stay the hell away from me." Inmate ask to see another nurse, who talk to her til about 3am. Inmate began telling me, they had swallowed some metal. I then observed them scraping the door, with a piece of metal. I told the inmate to give me the metal object. They stated "they need to protect them self, when someone came in their room on them. I'm still trying to get this metal object from them. They ask me if they could have a cup of coffee. I told them I would let them have coffee, if they gave me the metal object, lay down and go to sleep. The inmate gave me the object, I gave them the coffee, they drinked it, laid down and went to sleep. No more problems. I'm worn out mentally at this point. LOL

10/28/90 Security Supervisor – 2nd shift Capt. called and ask me could I come in, because the same inmate had been admitted to the outside hospital. I reported for duty, I saw the Lt. they stated to me "I got your book," "I was like what book?" The Lt. told me my wavier was approved to take the Sgt's examine, so they brought me their book. To the outside hospital with the same inmate, who is very manipulative and unpredictive, should be watch very close. The hand is always quicker than the eyes. Even with restraints on they would pick up shit. You wouldn't know it til later on. I Hated it when they were admitted at the outside hospital. It would drain you mentally, trying to keep up with this one and their shenanigans. They would come out the restraints, then you have to fight to get them back on them. While the other Officers would be dealing with this inmate and getting restraints back on them. I would stand back against the wall, due to being armed, securing other Officers weapons, while they dealt with the inmate.

10/29/90 Unit Infirmary – This inmate had been returned to the facility and was housed in Mental Health. We were informed inmate had several seizures. Oh Lawd, here we go back out to the hospital (smh) Inmate received medical care. I went out to the hospital, to assist with transporting the inmate back to the facility. Once we returned to the facility, inmate became uncooperative, because the Sgt was guiding them from behind. Inmate stated to the Sgt "she didn't want to show them what a nigger she was, just raising total hell at this point, stating "I'm not letting you take these restraints off, after you put me in that cell. Inmate still hostile, uncooperative was placed in the cell, sit on the bed, when they began spitting on staff, attempting to bite staff. Inmate was given medications, that calmed them down. All staff exited the cell.

11/01/90 1400 I received a call from day shift Lt. informing that PERT had been activated, not to leave town, give a number where I could be reached at all times. I received another phone call, to be at the facility at 2045 at the staff house in plain clothes. I arrived at the facility at 2030. I reported to my unit, the Lt. ask me What was I doing there? I told then I got a call from the other Lt. stating, be here at 2045. My Lt. stated "Ford! Sunday at 1045. I was told to be at the unit at 2045, they didn't say Sunday. I was off Saturday night, so I could report for duty for PERT, Sunday morning. 11/04/90 -1045 am I arrived at the unit, all management on location along with an outside Special agency. I was informed that a called was received from someone, who stated that someone was coming to bust an inmate out of the facility, with the aid of a semi-automatic weapon. Sunday about 0200 the subjects drove up to the facility down the hill. I observed one subject get out and start running, up the sidewalk to the front door of the facility. I heard a call over the radio, that the subjects were on the grounds. PERT stop them at the door. I came out the control center, proceeded to the office where the subject was being questioned. The subject continuously asking "what's going on" they wanted to make a call to their Lawyer. The subject was asked permission, to search their vehicle, they refused. The subject stated this was not their car, it was their roommate's. A call was made to the roommate, for permission to search their car, they also refused. The subject was then asked to step back out to their vehicle, at which time they were informed to leave the premises, do not come back. If seen on the premises, the police will be called, and they will be arrested & prosecuted for trespassing. 1620 Debriefed, I was told I would need to report for duty tonight at 2000 pm. 1700 I exited the facility. 2045 I report back for duty, my name was not called out for line up. Capt. ask me why was I at work? I told them I was following instructions, to report for duty. Capt. ask, "how long was I out there?" I told them and they stated "you work a couple of hours, leave at 0000 because the shift was covered. Working 8 hrs back then was a breeze. Loved working these hours 10-6, 6-2, and 2-10. There was not enough staff then, there is not enough now and it's probably going to be the same in the future.

12/07/90 Tower 1- I was relieved to transport an inmate out to the hospital. Inmate seem to be in a lot of pain, due to pregnancy. Upon the inmate being examined, we waited for the test results. Dr. in to talk with the inmate, so the inmate ask the Dr could they stay overnight? The DOC states how much it cost a day, to stay in the hospital. The inmate says, "it's the state money." The Doc stated No!! it's my money and their money. The inmate stated, "my insurance will pay for it." After the inmate made the Doc feel guilty as Hell, they decided they would let the inmate stay in the hospital, but they would be risking their job. I stated to the Doc, if there is no reason for them to stay in this hospital, they will go back to the facility. I talked to the inmate, who had a lot going on in their mind. The inmate calmed down after our talk. Doc proceeded with a few more tests, they told the inmate they would give them something for pain. We returned to the facility. Once we arrived another inmate was on their way out to have a baby.

12/21/90 Unit Infirmary – relieved 2nd shift, making security checks, conducting count. Several doors were unsecure, informed 2nd shift they need to secure doors before they leave. I ask the Officer why the inmates won't locked down, they stated "are they supposed to be locked down? "yes". As I continued to count the Officer comes out of the Mental Health area stating "I'm going home, "I told them we had to get the count. The Officer began walking towards the front, to exit stating to me "watch and see." I told them they could not leave, until I verified the count and the other Officers went out. I headed to the front to check the count with the door officer. The officer was out the door letting staff out. I told them you don't let anyone out until everything is verified, especially the count. This officer was acting really ignorant and pissed off, because I wouldn't let them out. I explained I knew they were ready to go home, but they would have to wait until, I clear the count. Meantime, the officer was standing halfway out the door. I'm still trying to get this damn count straight. Reported the incident to the Capt. Who states to make documentation? WOW! Well after all that drama, the most assaultive inmate housed in this area, woke up and was in discomfort, possible labor pains. Informed the Capt. They stated that, other staff was busy locking up an inmate.

Staff arrived to assist, inmate was checked out, they were having pains, but not labor pains.

1/02/91 Unit Infirmary – Unit Infirmary I was informed that there had been some problems with the inmates in the inpatient area. This was a 4bed suite. I conducted an in-house movement to try and keep down the drama. The inmate I moved was told by myself, if they had any problems, with the other inmates to come find me. Well another inmate started flapping them gums, stating to me they were no going to be worried tonight. I just starred at them and told them they need to go to bed. I was also informed that another inmate had attempted to take their self out earlier causing self-injury. Medical requested that I check inmate to make sure they had no objects on them. I informed the Officer at the door, what was going on, they act like they didn't want to be bothered, acting snobbish. REALLY!!! I'm trying to talk to them, and they couldn't look me in my damn face. How stupido can you get. A complete search was on the inmate who stated, "why I got to go through this shit again." Then an inmate in the inpatient area started acting a Buck, stating "close their door." The inmate was informed their door couldn't be closed inmate stated "well ya'll need to shut the fuck up. If I can't get any sleep, nobody else is going to sleep in this bitch."

1/05/91 Unit Infirmary- The Sgt was in the area earlier, looking for some property for an inmate, that they could not find. Later, the Sgt returned with another Officer to escort an inmate to lock up. The Sgt told me to call the dorm and have the Officer to meet them, at the gate and receive 2 safekeepers. The Officer stated that the floor Officer was making rounds. As I was telling the Sgt. The "bitch" hung up the phone up on me. I called them back and ask "why?" They stated, "I thought you were done," liar, liar. They still didn't meet me at the gate. I expressed to the Sgt "I was really sick of these ignorant ass Officers. They will need me before I need them, I promise you that."

1/17/91 Lock up – relieved 2ⁿᵈ shift, the inmates were requesting the Officer assigned to that hall, to light their cigarettes, the Officer refused. Inmates became loud and belligerent, beating and banging on their cell doors, cursing, hollering for grievances. I informed the Sgt office. The Sgt in the building making rounds, due to all the hell raising going on. There was Officers that would do things to aggravate the inmates and cause other staff to suffer the repercussion from their actions.

1/21/91 Tower 4 Training, Officer trained me how to make security checks of all these areas, at certain times. I received a call from Capt. who ask me, if I made the statement to anyone, to the effects of me being special. I was livid, Really Capt!!!They stated that someone told them, quote and unquote that Me, I said that if this particular inmate had to be transported to outside hospital, I knew I was going. I told the Capt. I don't even talk to these people here, because that's their MO to start trouble. I ain't got time for that. After that the Capt. had me running the grounds and doing escorts. Gofer LOL!

1/22/91 Unit Infirmary – 3 Officers assigned. Inmate began to complain about having stomach pains. The Officer that I was working with, told me, you know you are going out to the hospital. I told them "no, I was not." How about 5 mins later, the Sgt called and stated for me to transport an inmate. I was like DAMN!!! I was preparing the inmate to be transported, the inmate asks do she have to wear handcuffs. "Yes, you do that's policy. I was in ER all night with this inmate, due to no bed availability. The Sgt stated just stay at the hospital, until the inmate was placed in a room. That never happen so I was relieved by 1st shift.

1/23/91 dorm – 2 Officers with A, B,C hall downstairs. Relieved 2nd shift dorm just off the chain. Inmates downstairs standing in the doorway, before the count is cleared. Inmates on C hall was following me as I conducted the count. This is unreal, I told them they need to stay in place, until this count has cleared. There were 3 inmates in one room. I told them whoever did not belong in here, need to get to stepping. The inmates stated to me "we weren't doing anything but talking." I told them either you go to your room or the dayroom, they knew what the rules were. They said to me, "we can if we get permission, we can get a chair and sit out in the hall." "who you gone get permission from, I'm the Officer, I said No! you will not during my tour." Later, I went to make rounds downstairs and the inmates were sitting on the steps. I told them to "get off these steps." The inmates stated the Officers let us sit here, "well you want sit there tonight MOVE! The inmates said "we get told so many different things. I told them they know the rules better than I do. Bedtime inmates just everywhere, standing in the hallways talking. This dorm kept you busy the entire 8 hours. The other Officer received a call from the Sgt.to conduct a complete search on an inmate, just pick out an inmate. We did and told the inmate, we needed to conduct a complete search, of course the inmate started asking questions. "Why?" she wants to know where it came from. Who ordered the search? The inmate seems to be intimidated. I told them there was no need for them to feel intimidated. This was policy and we were going to do our jobs, get back in the bed and go to sleep, no problems other than them being pissed off. The Sgt was notified that the task was complete. Sgt called and requested we go and do breaks, be the Gofer, LOL

1/24/91 Tower 4 I was relieved and summoned to the infirmary, inmate in labor, had to be transported to outside hospital, cursing, raising hell. If anything happens to their baby, she was going to get all us mother fuckers. This inmate was cursing, bitching all the way to the hospital. The Sgt restrained the inmate's cuffs until we arrive at the ER. After convincing this convict to get in the wheelchair, we escorted them to labor and delivery area. The nurse stated that, they had a room already for the inmate. The inmate began asking for the Dr. from the unit. Medical told the inmate to put on the hospital gown, they jumped out the wheelchair and set in the chair, stating they were not doing anything until the Dr. got there, still raising hell. 10 mins later the Dr showed up and talked to the inmate, asking them what the problem was, as they were pulling off their draws. I just knew they was going to, throw them on one of us. Inmate didn't know what was going on, because they never had a baby before. It was determined that they were in labor. The inmate stated "someone need to get in contact with their family and tell them to bring their ass there and get their damn baby, their baby was not staying here, with these white blood sucking mother fuckers. The inmate was told, everything was being handled, by the Social Worker who later showed up. Key people from the facility showed up, because they knew the inmate was going to and did create havoc at that hospital.

1/26/91 Unit Infirmary I was sitting at the desk when I heard an inmate request, that their door be opened, medical stated to the inmate "say please." The inmate said, "please what?" Medical stated say please to show some curtorsey." The inmate said, "fuck that, I am choking to death in here." There again staff with bad judgement aggravating an inmate, that will cause, not them but someone else to be assaulted by this inmate.

1/28/91 Unit Infirmary – The Lt. called and stated for me to escort some inmates back to their dorms, in which I did. The Lt. told me when I returned, they would go with me to the infirmary to help assist with an inmate escort back to lock up. Returned and escort inmate to lockup and exited. The Sgt called requesting, I go to a dorm and conduct a strip search on an inmate, because the new Officer had never completed a strip search before. I entered the dorm, told inmate to get up and come down to the bathroom, of course they have questions "why?" I told inmate, let's just do it and get it over with. No one knows anything about this but us, a search was completed. I ask the Officer did they understand everything, did they have any questions, they stated "no." I then went to another dorm, where it appeared another inmate's water broke. The inmate stated they could not understand, why they had water coming down their legs. The inmate was escorted by way of wheelchair to medical. I went with the Lt. to another dorm, because the Officer was having problems with an inmate. I had the inmate to come out front so the Lt. could talk to them. The inmate did not want to take their meds, saying they were having bad dreams The Lt. and I tried very hard to convince this inmate to take their meds. The inmate stated that the other inmates were making fun of them, saying they are a mental patient. The inmate was scared to death of the LT. saying, "you gone put that grabbing wrist thing on my arm." Talking about IKKIYO unarm self-defense. The inmate would not go and receive their meds, because they stated they did not trust medical, they would give them a shot. The inmate was scared the Lt. was going to lock them up, after all this the inmate went back, got in bed. No more problems.

1/29/91 Relief Officer I was called to transport an inmate out to the hospital 4th floor triage. The inmate began to hound me about calling their family. They were told at the facility infirmary, that they were going to call. I told the inmate I had no knowledge of this. I would try and find out something, when I got back to the facility. I called to the facility and talked to the Capt., asking them if they knew anything about this inmate calling their family and they said "no." The only way their family would be notified, is a emergency situation. I told the inmate and they just kept going on and on, stating they need to contact their family and let the know what was going on. Finally, I just told them "don't ask me anymore." Dr. came in and ask me if they could speak to the inmate alone. "NO!" Then medical ask me "was there really anything wrong with them? O r were they using the pain, as an excuse to get out to the hospital, to use the phone. I stated I don't know that depends on what they find out. The same Dr. that saw the inmate a couple of days earlier, came back to see them again and determined "really, it too much." I returned to the facility. Later on that morning the Capt. Told me to go to another dorm, due to the same inmate that would not take their meds, walking around causing confusion in the building, saying to the Officer that they hated them. They dreamed they killed their mother. Scared the Officer to death. I finally convinced this convict to take their meds. I escorted inmate to mental health they received their meds. I escorted them back to their dorm.

2/17/91Unit Infirmary relieved 2nd shift the Sgt called and requested, I come to lock up to assist with an inmate getting meds. Upon going to the cell, the Sgt was talking to the inmate to the inmate, at the door about their meds. The cell door was opened, staff entered. The inmate stated "what all these Officer's doing in here? You don't need all these Officers." Once the inmate calmed down on their bed, medical entered with med in shot form. This convict refused stating "those shots hurt, "inmate stated they would take the meds in liquid form. Medical back to retrieve liquid meds, inmate just talking away. Medical returned with the meds. The inmate requested that; I pour liquid meds in their mouth. Now my thinking was they was going to spit this shit back at me, or someone else. I did give the inmate the meds, they took them without a problem. Whew! All staff exited. I returned to my assigned post. I received a call from the Sgt to go down to the dorm, relieve an Officer who stated, they had been trying to get in contact with a family member, they were not answering their phone. They wanted to go check on them and make sure they were ok. It was not like them, not to answer the phone. The Officer didn't know whether they would be back or not. It was later found out that the Officer's family member had falling, broke their hip and was lying on the floor not able to get up.

2/22/91 Sec Supervisor – I was sent out to supervise an inmate that had full blown HIV and possible meningitis. During the night, this inmate had thrown up, hawked stuff up so many times, just made me sick at my stomach. Then HIV, was a prevalent virus we all had to be careful of, not coming in contact with body fluids, around this time there were a lot of videos and classes to educate the public, about these different viruses. A lot of times you were around inmates that had these viruses, but you didn't know. You would take precautions all the time, probably when you didn't need to half the time. Even out in the free world you have to be careful with who you dealt with. You did it to protect yourself and the people around you. The inmates would let you know most of the time, saying "you might want to use some gloves" or they would just come right out and tell you, they had the virus. Working in this environment, you never knew what kind of issues you would be subjected to. Then I began to understand why staff was being offered Hepatitis vaccine shots, that were provided by the state and they did hurt. So, if you ever became sick or ill you will be covered by the stated, as far as medical time out of work. If you didn't take them and you got exposed, you were up the creek without a boat or a paddle.

Later on, down the road we would have to get tuberculosis (TB) screenings done every year.

3/07/91 Tower 1 / Gatehouse – Officer came out of the Control center to relieve and Officer to retrieve a wheelchair and go down to the dorm. The Capt. advised me that, I may be going out to the hospital ER, with an inmate in labor. Once I was relieved, I picked up my equipment, proceeded to the infirmary gate to pick up inmate. I arrived at ER, we proceeded inside, the inmate started having contractions, EMS attendant retrieved a wheelchair for me. Once the triage medical determined inmate was 5 centimeters. The inmate was transported to the 4th floor. I called back to the facility to give my location, for the next shift. During this time, we use the base station radios and car radios to communicate. You didn't have cell phones then. There were like bag phones that, you could utilize in the car if necessary. Now we got cellular phones and they do everything but walk. LOL I returned to the unit turned in my equipment and I'm outta here, headed to garner road YMCA to work out.

3/17/91 Tower 4 relieved 2nd shift making my security rounds. The Sgt called me by radio, I told them I would call them as soon as I got to a phone. When I arrived at Tower 1, there was a Sgt there relieving another Officer. When I ask what the Sgt wanted when they called me? I was told we were being summoned to mental health due to an inmate acting out, not complying. Inmate was crying and screaming, all they wanted was someone to talk to. There was another admissions inmate, we found out later the they were a master in Black Belt Karate. The inmate claimed their hands was registered as a deadly force, there story did check out, at least that's the information I received from my supervisors. This inmate we had to be very careful with, be mindful of who dealt with them on a daily basis.

3/20/19 Unit Infirmary – relieved 2nd shift They passed on that that, they had one inmate giving them problems all day, they were not to be out of their room. This was the first thing I observed, this inmate out of their room after being advised, not to exit their room. I told them not to come out that room again. The inmate started talking about their belongings, the Sgt said they could have them. The inmate stated they were going to the outside hospital and they needed their eyebrow pencil and makeup. The Lt. in building to make rounds and talked to this strumpet. The inmate told the Lt. they were going to sign a refusal to go out to hospital, if they could not get their makeup. I was sent out to the hospital with a new officer and a crazy close custody inmate. I was told by the Capt., I was the Lead Officer, show the new staff what to do. Hell, I was the only Officer.

3/25/19 Unit Infirmary Door – The Sgt in with a New Admission to be assess. Inmate sitting in chair looking very paranoid. Staff attempted to talk to the inmate. Obviously, they didn't want to talk, about whatever was going on with them. Inmate was escorted back to dorm lockup. Capt. Called and ask me to work my night off Friday, stating they would give me Monday as a comp night.

3/26/19 Tower 4 – I was informed by another Officer that in the stockroom, by the steps the wood door was missing the lock. The key to the stockroom door was about to break. I obtain another key from the Sgt. I went inside the door of the stockroom, to pick up bed packs for the dorm. This was all the new admissions and safekeepers were housed at the time. I assisted another Officer in moving mattresses to cells for admissions and safekeepers. I had to pick up blankets for Single Cell. After all this was completed, the Sgt and I went to the dining hall to pick up Ramadan which was distributed to the dorms then.

3/28/19 Unit Infirmary – I was called out by the Sgt to conduct some escorts to pick up inmates for meds. I was taken inmates back to Single Cell, Oh My God! There was a SNAKE. I don't do snakes. I notified the Sgt; they came and killed the snake. I had received a call from another Sgt to go to one of the dorms, show the Officer how to do a complete search. I received a call again stating, one had to go out to the hospital, to have a baby, their water broke. I went and picked up my equipment. The Sgt said the inmate was honor grade inmate, stay with inmate until they are admitted, call back with info. I returned to the facility, turned in equipment.

3/30/19 Mental Health – I had left about 2:30 to go check the warehouse, for an inmate's belongings, because they had been released on bond. When I arrived back to the area, the Officer had not completed my 141's. I told medical the next time I leave, I would leave my 141's with them, so they could keep them up for me. The Officer got upset, but do you think I care. You get what you give. I had an inmate standing at the cell door, talking about they had some apple jack. I was like "what the hell is they talking about?" It was rolled up dry apple peeling, just like a joint. The inmate told me they were going to get "fucked up." I ask medical, could you get high off dry apple peel and they said "yes." I went and obtain this item from the inmate. I notified the Sgt, they told me to "throw that shit away," but of course I kept it for future references.

3/31/19 Unit Infirmary – I was training a new officer what to do in the area. When the Sgt called stating that, they were sending another Officer, so the new staff could be in the inpatient area. The Officer arrived took over the door and the keys. The phone rings at the door, no answer, so they call me. The staff stated to me that the new Officer needs to stay at the front by the phone. They had been trying to call and no one was answering. I told the Officer that, the other Officer had the keys. There was staff standing at the gate waiting to get in. I informed the staff; I did not have the key. I can't help that, plus I couldn't find them. The Officer was at the other gate waiting on medical, who went to distribute meds. The Officer that called had a bad attitude; I just could really care less. The Sgt called and told me to go pick up an inmate that supposedly been bitten, by something. That morning my relief came, I was giving my report for the night, the Officer left with the new staff. I was coming up the sidewalk, the Sgt was leaving, they ask me where was the new staff, I told them gone with the other Officer, on their way out gate. The Sgt stated "they know better, you all are supposed to leave together. When I got out to the parking lot, I told the Officer about it, they stated they were not going to wait for me, because I was back there running my mouth. I said nothing else. The Sgt stated I will tell them, if it doesn't do any good, to let them know. Yeah Right!

6/24/19 I was security Supervisor relief Officer. I relieved an Officer that was sitting with an inmate in the ER, that had been in a fight in the dorm, they had cuts on their back from getting push through a glass.

7/22/19 Tower 1 I relieved 2nd shift My Sgt told me, I needed to leave work at 3 am for comp time, due to being sec sup for 3 nights at the hospital. Then the Capt. turned right around and ask me to work my night off. Working wasn't an issue. I didn't like the comp time. LOL

8/15/91 My first day working at Raleigh Durham Airport for CCS Security. I worked one week to be exact. I was supposed to be part time. They had me working 40 hrs a week 8am-5pm. I was working night shift from 10pm-6am. I couldn't make it after I worked that Friday, I did not return. Once I quit, they called me and said a part time position came open, but that I had quit to soon. I told then I could not burn the candle at both ends. I was not going to jeopardize my primary job.

8/22/91 Dorm B1 – The Capt. was asking about an inmate's belongings, that could not be found. The Sgt and I look over that entire compound, The Capt. told me to write a statement concerning the matter. The Sgt ask another Officer about doing the inventory and they stated they could not remember, doing inventory for that inmate. I told the Sgt the Officer was a "lie" because we did the inventory together. "That's why I kept note."

They talk junk about me and my notebook, but I can tell you what you needed to know. So, don't go to sleep on me. LOL!

8/24/91 Dorm B1 I was sent to the Tower to relieve 2nd shift Officer until another Officer, who was late came in. When I returned to B1 there were a lot of inmates up. I had an inmate to come to the gate and ask, could they come out to the TV area. I told them No!, you should have come out before the gate closed at 11:30. Lots of inmates were going to bed, back talking in the bed area, disturbing other inmates, who were sleeping. I told them if they did not go to bed, I would start writing them up. Back then inmates lobby hours were 2:00am through the weekdays, holidays and weekends it was on, they could be up in the lobby all night, of course you know you would have those inmates that took advantage of this time.

8/25/91 Dorm B1 relieved 2nd shift 79 inmates assigned. Inmates in shorts again. An inmate asks the other Officer to remove an inmate, who was housed on A side to B side that, was at the card table playing cards. The inmate had a nerve to get pissed off, when they figured out this was not Burger king and they could not have it their way. I informed them of the rules, 2nd shift Officer was gone for the night, they best get right!

8/27/91 Dorm B2 It's so funny, cause through all this, everything we do now is done on the computers and laptops, then it was done manually. You actually had to be able to add and subtract. You didn't get to use a calculator, only in the control center. WOW! You had to actually add numbers and subtract numbers. Now the calculator does it, which became a crutch for many. Who remembers AOL- America On Line? This was the biggest and the only online provider that we had. I guess it's still there. These other online providers came along and stole the thunder from AOL. Technology has come a long way, since then. Hell, you couldn't even go home and go to sleep, without getting on line. Now it's worse, it's right there in our hands. It has us so preoccupied that we can't pay attention!!! NCCIW use to get the newspaper daily and on Sundays everyone remembers them COUPONS!!! LOL. I don't even think they deliver anymore. How many remember the Thom Joyner SKY show, follow by Women's Empowerment should be about 30 years old now.

8/29/91 Tower 1 relieved 2nd shift Officer, it was a key missing. The Officer didn't seem to know where the key was. I notified the OIC, they came over and tried to locate the key. I told the Officer they couldn't go anywhere, until those keys were accounted for. There was a note in the key box, the keys had been signed out by Lt. and Sgt.

9/4/91 Lock up dorm – The Lt. ask me to work Saturday night. I told them; I couldn't work. They stated to me "some damn body gotta work. " I told them if they couldn't get anyone else to work, I would work.. There was an Officer that wanted to work on Saturday and be off on Sunday. I informed the Lt. and they made the change.

9/5/91 Unit Infirmary This night we were so short staff, that the Sgts were escorting inmates back and forth from various dorms. Two new admissions were brought in that night, one was 16-year-old who had shot her 50-year-old boyfriend.

9/8/91 assigned Dorm I received a call from the Sgt asking me where was I at Friday. I told them; I was at home. They stated to me that administration was trying to contact me, for a Sgts interview.

9/10/91 Dorm B2 Dorm had been sprayed for lice, some of the inmate's clothes were out at the stockroom being washed and dried. The Sgt was going to check on the clothes and bring them up, when they finished. Inmates asking for blankets, I told then if I gave one blanket out, then everyone was going to want a blanket. I could not provide extra blankets. I couldn't do for one that I could not do for all. Sgt called and gave me a list of inmates that would be transferring. Myself along with another Officer finished inventorying about 1:00 am. Officer outside B1 killing a snake and the Lt. was running. LOL I was then called to transport an inmate to the outside hospital. Inmate was treated and returned to the facility.

9/14/91 dorm B2 Escorted several inmates to the unit infirmary for meds. The inmates began to argue with each other, both inmates escorted to the Sgts office. I then proceeded to the next dorm, to pick up an inmate who got busted by the Officer, with a big hunk of cheese from the dining room. Inmate claimed they got the cheese from another inmate, who was on the diet line. The cheese was destroyed, and the inmate was returned to their dorm.

10/14/91 Dorm B2 10:43 pm medical called and ask me did I have this inmate in my building. I told them "yes" then they ask me, to speak to the inmate. I explained to medical, that inmates are not authorized to talk on my telephone, they put another medical staff on the phone, and I explained the same thing to them. Medical stated they just talk to an inmate in dorm A2. I told them I would have to have permission. I called the Sgt informed them and they told me don't worry about it, they would take care of it. Then medical called back, requesting that I pass on some information to the inmate about their medicine.

10/15/91 dorm B1 The Lt informed me that PERT was on alert and would I get in contact with the members and let them know. There was an inmate due to be executed on Friday at 2:00am.

10/18/91 Security Supervisor – relieved the Sgt and 2 Officers in ER police room. The Sgt called us outside, stating they had been wrestling with this inmate all day, they are strong as a bull. LOL The inmate had wires paperclips or something they had inserted in their vagina. They were going to let the Dr get them out. REALLY!!! Inmate sitting in the police room with their head lying on the table. After sitting there for about an hour, come to find out 2nd shift didn't turn the sheet in, that supposed to be carried to the front for admissions. I ask the hospital security to check with the front desk to see, if they knew we were here, which they did not. So finally, we were called back to ER. Medical enter and tried to do a rectal examine on inmate. Medical was so hostile, X-rays were conducted, the objects were pass the inmate's birth canal. Medical came in with these long forcep looking things, like scissors. The Dr says to the inmate "I didn't put this in you, you did it yourself, I don't care if they rot, it don't make me no difference, so turn." Inmate did as instructed, the Dr was so pissed off, they told the nurse to write down refusal for rectal examine. Medical was so unprofessional and nasty. They did not know this inmate like we did. If they had of went off. I would have let them beat their asses, because of the way they treated them. Let them call Raleigh police, to get them off of them. The other Officer and I stood on each side of them restraining, their hands to keep them from knocking the hell out of someone. So, the Dr. and the nurse left mad. Then someone come in wanting the inmate to sign a paper for a follow up examine at the facility. Inmate was then returned to the facility and their housing unit Mental Health Informed staff of what occurred, and they ask how the inmate do. Inmate did well under the circumstances, of how they were treated. They did DAM good I then reported the incident to my supervisors.

10/22/91 Security Supervisor Here we go again!! SMH inmate out to hospital, to deliver their baby. Relieved 2nd shift, medical was administering a shot to the inmate, when the inmate hollered out "what are you sticking me with?" 10:45 inmate buzzed medical, asking for some Mylanta. Medical left a crack in the door, inmate hollering "close my door. "OH lawd! Medical had shift change, then another staff came in and turned the light on, inmate start hollering, "turn my damn light out." The inmate was loud that they startled the staff. Medical told the inmate they need to get their vitals and they could not see without some light. Inmate then stated "close my damn door, you are standing up in here looking stupid. "Staff ask "are you refusing to have your vitals taken, sre you refusing, to have your baby monitored, " inmate "obviously, get out of my room, close my door." Then the inmate went on and on about "you call who you want," just saying stuff to hear their self-talk, at this point I was the only one in the room. I know they want talking to me. I ask them "what are you hollering about?" Inmate states: close my fucking door, all I want you to do is close my fucking door." I told the inmate they need to shut their mouth up and stop all that hollering and being loud. Inmate stated, "I don't give a fuck, leave the mother fucker open." I was not going to allow them to run me out this room, because they could not have what they wanted, when they want it. When the inmate shut their mouth, I walked out the room and closed the door. No more problems for a little while, then they started again. I was so glad to be relieved to go home; I didn't know what to do.

10/24/91 Dorm B1 — In to see the Lt. who informed me to be at the facility Monday 28, 1991 at 12:00 noon dressed in PERT blues, for a farewell to the Superintendent and assistant. I was to get in contact with everyone on 3rd shift and let them know. I was assisting with transfers, inventorying inmate property. One inmate stated to tell the Sgt., it was against their best interest to be transferred. The Sgt stated to the inmate "you can pack your shit up to transfer or go to lock up, either way their belongings was going to be inventoried. The inmate is now on their way to lockup, for refusing to transfer. Then I had to go to Mental Health, this inmate had shit, all over the walls, floor and their hands, pee smelling, and we had to go in so medical could check their knee and clean up some of that mess she made. SHIT was everywhere!!! There was this one inmate we would always have to deal within a constant basis, from self-mutilation, assaultive behavior and cursing out staff, to putting stuff in their body cavities. This inmate was the inmate of all inmates LOL. They would make statements like "y'all mother fuckers are not going home today." To be show, this inmate would do something off the chain, and we would be right there at that prison. This inmate would say "I told y'all bitches you won't going home" and they would be laughing. This inmate had returned to prison 2 or 3 times, an inmate that was caught in what we call a revolving door. I remember they told me one time, they were there because they stole the Police car, they were driving around while they chased them. That was the funniest thing to them. I ask them "why you steal the police car." They stated, "their dumb ass left the keys in the car." This was a very manipulative inmate, there was a special cell made just for them, with an extended trap door. If they said they were going to get you, they try to make well on their threats. This was the only cell they could be placed in.

We did have hard to manage inmates, some of the staff, was not comfortable dealing with them. I would always remind staff as I travel through the rank, you can say or do what you see me do. I have been here for some time and gained respect from most of these ladies. That's something you can incur only with time. You can't come in gun hoe and think it all about you and the uniform. You must give respect to gain respect. Working in Corrections has taught me a lot of lessons. I learned from some of the best teachers, with my successes and downfalls. Those experiences help to create who I became. You try and make every day count. Take a bad day and try to turn it into a good day, appreciate every moment, take everything from it that you can. If it had not been for my faith, trust and love in the Lord Savior Jesus Christ, I know for a fact I would not be where I am. I give him praises every day, I wake up and have breath in my body. I know I would not have made it and continue to push forwarded, without him in my life.

Down through the years I have seen, heard and been through a lot. During that time, it made me strong and built my **resilience.** I have come to believe that things happen to you in life, were meant to happen at that given moment. Everything happens for a reason, whether it's good, bad, ugly, illness, injury, love, last moments or just stupidity. We don't know why it happens, but a lot of things that happen test your mind, body and soul. The old saying is live everyday like it's your last day. As Forest Gump could say "life is like a box of chocolates, because we don't know how long we will be in this life. If we knew the people in the world would be in pure havoc and pandemonium. My Mom use to say to me, the day you were born, a date was marked on the calendar, of how long you would be in this life. It could be seconds, minutes hours, days, weeks or year.

This is a card that I receive from a staff person who moved on from NCCIW:

Capt. Ford,

You are a person with a good heart. I am glad for the time that I had working for you and for that time, I have had to talk to ya about life in general. You truly touch others w/your kindness and your leadership skills and that's something very special.

I had some very good staff, some good staff and the not so good staff. When you have staff that follow through with their jobs or assignments, you don't have to say anything, because they already know what need to be done, this made a great day when everything just falls in place, cause for less stress. Then you have staff that you have instruct them from point A-Z what need to be done. I was not a micro manager. When I went through the rank Officer, Sergeant, Lieutenant, Unit Manager and Captain I did not like to be micromanaged. I knew what to do and followed through with my job duties, unless my supervisors, ask me to complete duties or a task I had no knowledge of. Then you have the staff that know everything and know nothing, half of the time getting in trouble, because they "ASSUME." I've done that to Assume and I learned my lesson. The new staff that came on board, out of 10% of them, I would say 6% maybe would listen and the others would be in their own little world. You can't come to work in this type of environment and be undue. The word undue is very broad. It can mean so many things. My Mom always told me "don't sleep were you work; it will cause so many problems." Some staff get hired and come in, they already know what's up and their mind set. A lot of staff that come in DOC come to begin a career. Don't come in and get drawn into the drama. Working in prison you don't have any friends, you have associates. You began working, starting off at a good point, don't allow other staff make you become who they are disgruntle, no respect, disrespected and don't care attitudes. You will not travel far, if you do it will not be a good ride, I promise you. Reporting for duty, we have to be sound of mind, have morale values, be prepared for anything. We are there to do a job.

12/31/15 was my last working day with the department of corrections. Let me tell you something, the day I walked out of there, it was a great feel of relief. 1/1/116 New Years! was my first day as a retired employee. I made it yall!!! Such a wonderful feeling. Even though I still have to remind myself, that I am retired. I continue to work my part time jobs, to stay busy. I did not want to go home and sit down, watch the walls and become a couch potato. This would literally drive me insane. I have missed working at the prison communicating with coworkers and inmates, even though some did not care for me. LOL YESSSS! I miss that adrenaline rush. Well now the prisons are being staff with millennials (technology) generation, very few old school staff, the one that are still there and trying to leave as soon as they can in some form or fashion. When I retired, I had all these thoughts built up in my head. I had to have a way to get rid of it mentally, so this is some of why I wrote the book to. There have been so many things that has happen since my departure. I pray for my fellow coworker's every day, that they remain safe, always watch your back, be conscious of your surroundings at work and away from work. Life is precious, enjoy every day like it's your last. We are here one minute and gone the next. We don't know the time, day, hour or second. One thing for sure and two things for certain, we all are going to leave this earth. This is part of my story. I have already started another book called (back) in the day, coming soon.

CPSIA information can be obtained
at www.ICGtesting.com
Printed in the USA
LVHW022354060621
689439LV00001B/23